THE MAID, THE MILLIONAIRE AND THE BABY

MICHELLE DOUGLAS

MILLS & BOON

First published in Great Britain 2019
by Mills & Boon, an imprint of HarperCollins*Publishers*
1 London Bridge Street, London, SE1 9GF

Large Print edition 2020

© 2019 Michelle Douglas

ISBN: 978-0-263-08452-8

MIX
Paper from
responsible sources
FSC
www.fsc.org   FSC™ C007454

This book is produced from independently certified
FSC™ paper to ensure responsible forest management. For
more information visit www.harpercollins.co.uk/green.

Printed and bound in Great Britain
by CPI Group (UK) Ltd, Croydon, CR0 4YY

For Millie,
who is ever-generous with her smiles. We're
so happy to welcome you to the family.

CHAPTER ONE

IMOGEN ADJUSTED HER earbuds, did a quick little shimmy to make sure they weren't going to fall out and then hit 'play' on the playlist her father had sent her. She stilled, waiting for the first song, and then grinned at the sixties Southern Californian surf music that filled her ears.

Perfect! Threading-cotton-through-the-eye-of-a-needle-first-time perfect. Here she was on an island, a slow thirty-minute boat ride off the coast of Brazil, listening to surf music. She pinched herself. Twice. And then eyed the vacuum cleaner at her feet, reminding herself that she was here for more than just tropical holiday fun. A detail that was ridiculously difficult to bear in mind when everywhere she looked she was greeted with golden sand, languid palm trees, serene lagoons and gloriously blue stretches of perfect rolling surf.

Still, in a few hours she could hit the beach, or go exploring through the rainforest, or...

Or maybe find out what was wrong with her aunt.

Her smile slipped, but she resolutely pushed her shoulders back. She'd only been here for three days. There was time to get to the bottom of whatever was troubling Aunt Katherine.

Switching on the vacuum cleaner, she channelled her inner domestic goddess—singing and dancing as she pushed the machine around the room. This was the *only* way to clean. Housework was inevitable so you might as well make it as fun as you could.

She'd been *so* quiet for the last three days, but the lord of the manor, Jasper Coleman, didn't like noise, apparently.

Each to his own.

She shrugged, but the corners of her mouth lifted. At eleven o'clock every day, however, he went for an hour-long run. A glance at her watch told her she had another fifty minutes in which to live it up before she'd have to zip her mouth shut again and return to an unnatural state of silence—and in which to dust, vacuum and tidy his living and dining rooms, his office and the front entrance hall. She meant to make the most of them.

She glanced around at the amazing beach-house mansion. While she might refer to Jasper Coleman as lord of the manor, his house didn't bear the slightest resemblance to an English manor house. The wooden beams that stretched across the vaulted ceilings gave the rooms a sense of vastness—making her feel as if she were cast adrift at sea in one of those old-fashioned wooden clippers from the B-grade pirate movies starring Errol Flynn and Burt Lancaster that she used to love so much when she was a kid. A feeling that was solidly countered by the honey-coloured Mexican tiles that graced the floors, and the enormous picture windows that looked out on those extraordinary views.

She angled the vacuum cleaner beneath the coffee table. She should *love* this house. But the artfully arranged furniture and designer rugs looked like something out of a lifestyle magazine for the rich and famous. Everything matched. She repressed a shudder. Not a single thing was out of place.

Now if *she* owned the house… *Ha! As if.* But if she did, it'd look vastly different. Messier for a start. Her smile faded. There were shadows in this house, and not the kind she could scrub off the walls or sweep out of the door. No wonder Aunt Katherine had become so gloomy.

And those two things—Aunt Katherine and gloomy—just didn't go together. The weight she'd been trying to ignore settled on her shoulders. She had to get to the bottom of that mystery, and not just because she'd promised her mother. Aunt Katherine was one of her favourite people and it hurt to see her so unhappy.

Another surfing song started and she kicked herself back into action. She had a house to clean, and she'd achieve nothing by becoming gloomy herself. She turned the music up and sang along as if her life depended on it, wiggling her backside in time with the music and twirling the vacuum cleaner around like an imaginary dance partner. While the rooms might be tidy, they were huge, and she had to get them done before Mr Coleman returned and locked himself away again in his office to do whatever computer wizardry he spent his days doing. In a suit jacket! Could you believe that? He wore a suit jacket to work here on an island that housed precisely four people. Just…wow.

The second song ended and her father's voice came onto the recording. This was one of the joys of her father's playlists—the personal messages he tucked away in among the songs. 'We miss you, Immy.'

She rolled her eyes, but she knew she was grinning like crazy. 'I've only been gone three days.' She switched off the vacuum cleaner, chuckling at one of his silly stories involving the tennis club. He recommended a movie he and her mother had seen, before finishing with, 'Love you, honey.'

'Love you too, Dad,' she whispered back, a trickle of homesickness weaving through her, before a movement from the corner of her eye had her crashing back to the present. She froze, and then slowly turned with a chilling premonition that she knew who'd be standing there. And she was right. There loomed Jasper Coleman, larger than life, disapproval radiating from him in thick waves, and her mouth went dry as she pulled the earbuds from her ears.

Her employer was a huge bear of a man with an air of self-contained insularity that had the word *danger* pounding through her. A split second after the thought hit her, though, she shook herself. He wasn't *that* huge. Just…*moderately* huge. It was just… He was one of those men whose presence filled a room. And he filled this room right up to its vaulted ceiling.

A quick sweep of her trained dressmaker's eyes put him at six feet one inch. And while his shoulders were enticingly broad, he wasn't some barrel-chested, iron-pumping brawn-monger. Mind you, he didn't have a spare ounce of flesh on that lean frame of his, and all of the muscles she could see—and she could see quite a lot of them as he'd traded in his suit jacket for running shorts and a T-shirt—were neatly delineated. *Very* neatly delineated. *That* was what gave him an air of barely checked power.

That and his buzz cut.

So…not exactly a bear. And probably not dangerous. At least not in a 'tear one from limb to limb' kind of way. None of that helped slow the pounding of her pulse.

'Ms Hartley, am I right in thinking you're taking personal calls during work time?'

He had to be joking, right? She could barely get a signal on her mobile phone. She started to snort but snapped it short at his raised eyebrow. It might not be politic to point that out at this precise moment. 'No. *Sir,*' she added belatedly. But she said it with too much force and ended up sounding like a sergeant major in some farcical play.

Oh, well done, Imogen. Why don't you click your heels together and salute too?

'Not a phone call. I was listening to a playlist

my father sent me. He's a sound engineer…and he leaves little messages between songs…and I talk back even though I know he can't hear me. So…' She closed her eyes.

Too much information, Immy.

'I expected your aunt to have made it clear to you that I demand peace and quiet when I'm working.'

Her eyes flew open. 'She did!' She couldn't get Aunt Katherine into trouble. 'But, you see, I thought you'd already left for your run.'

She glanced at his office door and had to fight the urge to slap a hand to her forehead. She was supposed to check if that door was open or closed. Open meant he was gone and she could clean this set of rooms without disturbing him. If it was closed that meant he was still working… and she had to be church-mouse quiet. Biting her lip, she met his gaze again. 'I'm sorry. I forgot to check your office door. It won't happen again, Mr Coleman, I promise.'

He didn't reply. Nothing. Not so much as a brass razoo. Which was an odd expression. She'd look it up…if she could get an Internet connection. She eyed him uncertainty. He might not be a big bear of a man, but he fitted her image of a bear with a sore head to a T. Which might not be fair as she didn't know him, but she wasn't predisposed to like him either, the horrid old Scrooge.

He turned away, and she sagged with the relief of being released from those icy eyes. But then he swung back, and she went tense and rigid all over again. 'I'm going for my run *now*, Ms Hartley. In case my attire had slipped your attention.'

His sarcasm stung. Her fingers tightened about the vacuum cleaner, and suddenly it was Elliot's voice, Elliot's mocking sarcasm, that sounded through her head. She thrust out her chin. 'Did you just call me stupid?' She might only be the maid, but she didn't have to put up with rudeness. 'Look, I made a mistake and I apologised. It doesn't mean I'm stupid.'

'Oh, Imogen!' She could practically hear her mother's wail. *'What about Aunt Katherine? You promised!'*

Jasper Coleman had been in the act of moving towards the front door, but he turned back now with intimidating slowness. Rather than back down—which, of course, would be the sensible thing to do—she glared right back at him. She knew she might be a little too sensitive on the topic of her sharpness of mind and her reason—her *intelligence*—but she wasn't being paid enough to put up with derogatory comments directed at it.

At least, that was what she told herself before she started quaking in her sensible ballet flats. Her sense of self-righteousness dissolved as Jasper drew himself up to his full height. Any idiot knew you didn't go poking bears.

'I don't know you well enough to make a judgement call on your intelligence, Ms Hartley.' He gestured to his office door. 'A question mark does, however, hang over your powers of observation.'

She bit her tongue and kept her mouth firmly shut. Thankfully it appeared that he didn't expect an answer, as, without any further ado, he strode from the room. A moment later she heard the click of the front door closing. He didn't do anything as uncouth as slam it.

'Of course your attire hadn't slipped my attention,' she muttered, pushing her earbuds into the pocket of her skirt. She was a dressmaker. She noticed what everyone wore.

Though for some reason she'd *really* noticed what he'd been wearing. Which didn't make a whole lot of sense because his attire had been so very generic. Those nondescript running shorts had come to mid-thigh and were neither ridiculously tiny nor ridiculously tight. His T-shirt, though, had hugged his frame as if it'd been spray-painted on, highlighting the flex and play of firm muscle.

Oh, Imogen, who are you trying to kid?

It wasn't his clothes but the body inside the clothes that had held her attention so avidly.

Scowling, she pushed the image of her perplexing boss from her mind and completed the rest of the cleaning as quickly as possible, vacuuming and dusting immaculate surfaces. But, as her aunt said, they were immaculate because they were cleaned five days a week. Without fail. Because it was what the lord of the manor decreed, apparently.

Jasper's office was as immaculate as the rest of the house. And just as cold. Unlike her workspace at home, he didn't have any photographs sitting on his desk, no sentimental knick-knacks or anything personal. His room was functional and blank. He was supposed to be some kind of computer *wunderkind*, though how on earth he could create in a space that was so *beige* was beyond her.

She gave a final flick of her duster to the enormous desk, glanced around the room with a critical eye, and was about to leave when her gaze shifted to his computer…for the third time in about as many minutes. She bit her lip. She'd bet—given all the fancy tech gadgetry he had in here—he could log onto the Internet without a single problem.

She'd been trying to find out—for three days now—if the waters surrounding the island were safe. Aunt Katherine had no idea. She preferred the calm waters of the lagoon to the surf.

Jasper swam in his twenty-five-metre pool twice a day—from six to seven each morning and again in the evening. The man was obviously a fitness freak—three hours of cardio a day. Imagine? 'Kill me now,' she muttered. Not that she disapproved of fitness. She just couldn't do fitness for fitness's sake. She had to do something fun or it just wouldn't happen. Give her a Zumba or dance class, or the surf. She loved swimming in the ocean.

If it was safe.

Not giving herself any time to hesitate, she slid into her boss's chair, woke his computer from sleep mode and clicked the Internet browser icon. Surely he wouldn't mind? It'd be in his best interests to keep his staff safe, right? Occupational health and safety and all that.

She recalled the look in his eyes less than

thirty minutes ago, and her own churlish, 'Did you just call me stupid?' and grimaced. He might make an exception in her case and feed her to the sharks.

'So just hurry up and find out what you need to find out,' she ordered, typing in: Swimming in Brazilian waters.

The search engine results loaded onto the screen. 'Eureka.'

She leaned forward, intent on clicking the link to a website that looked as if it would give her the information she needed.

'Do *not* move a muscle, Ms Hartley,' a deceptively soft voice said from the doorway.

Imogen froze. She moved nothing but her eyes to meet her employer's gaze. 'Is there…?' She swallowed. 'Is there a snake or a scorpion about to pounce on me?' Her voice came out hoarse, but she was too afraid to cough and clear her throat in case she incited some animal to attack.

'Don't be ludicrous. Of course there isn't. Unless you call yourself a scorpion or a snake,' he added, striding towards her with a purposeful step, his lips pressed into a thin line.

Danger. The word whipped through her for the second time. This man was dangerous. She should've followed her first instincts. Leaping to her feet, she shot around the farthest side of the desk, keeping its wide expanse between them. She grabbed a paperweight in one hand, and then seized a pen and held it like a dagger in her other.

He slammed to a halt so quickly he swayed where he stood. 'What are you doing?'

'I don't like the look in your eyes.'

For some reason, her words made him pale. His chest lifted as he dragged in a breath. 'I don't like undercover journalists.'

'I'm not a journalist,' she spluttered, 'undercover or otherwise!'

'I hold the same contempt for industrial spies.'

She pointed the pen at his computer. 'You think I'm snooping in your personal files or... or your work files?'

Lips that shouldn't look quite so full twisted. 'The thought had crossed my mind.'

Wow, was this man paranoid or what? No wonder he lived on a desert island. And no wonder her aunt had warned her to be circumspect around him—*difficult* and *temperamental* had been the words she'd used.

'We seem to be at an impasse, Ms Hartley. I never for one moment meant for you to think that you were in physical danger from me.'

Oddly enough, she believed him.

'But I want to look at that computer screen to see precisely what it was that had you grinning like a Cheshire cat and shrieking "Eureka".'

That was probably a very good idea. 'How about I go this way until I'm standing in front of your desk?'

'And I'll go this way—' he gestured in the opposite direction '—until I'm behind my desk.'

'I want it on record that I take exception to the charge of shrieking, Mr Coleman. I don't shriek.'

'Duly noted, Ms Hartley.'

'Right, well…let's call that Plan A, shall we?' Imogen Hartley's lips lifted, but that didn't assuage the acid burning in Jasper's gut. The fear in her eyes as he'd started towards her had nearly felled him. What kind of brute did she take him for?

'Do you want me to count?' He didn't want to give her any further cause for alarm. 'On the count of three—'

With a frown in her eyes, as if he puzzled her, she shook her head and started moving around the desk. He kept his own steps measured and unhurried as he moved in the opposite direction.

Once they'd switched places, rather than looking meek and mild, or guilty and ashamed,

Imogen Hartley made an exaggerated flourish towards the computer like a model in an infomercial.

He muffled a sigh and took his seat. At least she didn't look frightened any more. Steeling himself, he turned to his computer. He stared at it for several long moments, blinked, and then eased back, his shoulders unhitching. 'You're checking the surf conditions?'

She nodded.

He tried to keep a frown from forming. 'Did you really think Ilha do Pequeno Tesoura—' he used the full Portuguese name of the island '—would be in the database of some surfing website?'

'Well, no, not exactly. But we're only a leisurely thirty-minute boat ride from the coast. Which means it'd be quicker by speedboat,' she added with a shrug, as if that explained everything.

A speedboat would reach the island in less than fifteen minutes. And her shrug explained nothing.

'So I thought that checking the surfing conditions on the coast might tell me what I needed to know.'

'Which is?'

She gestured, presumably towards the Atlantic Ocean on display outside his office window. 'If it's safe for me to swim on your beach.'

'Why?'

Two vertical lines appeared on her brow as if he'd just asked the most ridiculous question ever put to her—as if two seconds ago she'd considered him a sensible man and now she didn't.

Two minutes ago, she'd thought him a scary man. He'd never forgive himself for that.

Still, those lines on her brow were oddly cute… and kind of disturbing. Disturbing in the same way that seeing her dancing and singing while she'd been vacuuming had been disturbing. This woman was full of life and energy and spontaneity—full of unguarded reactions. It reminded him of normal people, and the outside world, and life. It was why he'd been so unforgivably short with her. The ache she'd unknowingly created inside him—an ache he'd thought he'd mastered a long time ago—had taken him off guard. It was why he'd come back early from his run—so he could ask Katherine to apologise to the girl on his behalf.

Apologise yourself now.

He opened his mouth. He closed it again. Katherine had rolled her eyes when she'd spoken of her niece—had said she was flighty and impulsive…recovering from the latest in a string of unsuitable relationships…had hinted, without saying as much, that her niece would find him irresistibly attractive. Be that as it may, while she might be irresponsible this girl was untouched by all the ugliness that surrounded him. And he'd like to keep it that way. It'd be better for all concerned if she considered him a temperamental grump rather than a reasonable human being.

He watched, fascinated, as she forced her face into polite lines. 'The reason I was checking the surf conditions is because I want to swim on the beach out there. My aunt couldn't tell me. She doesn't like the surf. If she wants a dip, she swims in the lagoon. You only swim in your pool. So…'

It took an effort of will not to lean towards her. 'So?'

'So I wondered if there was something wrong with it. Is there a great white shark colony camped just off the reef? Are there hidden rips or strange jellyfish? I mean, I've not noticed anything unusual, but…'

She trailed off with a shrug, her meaning clear. She'd evidently grown up with the same 'swim safe' messages that he and most other Australian children grew up with. The main beach here on Tesoura was a sheltered haven with rolling breakers created by the offshore reef, but the thought of her swimming alone disturbed him. 'Are you an experienced surfer?'

'I'm not a board rider, but I swim a lot at the local beaches back home.'

He searched his mind for where it was that Katherine's family called home.

'Wollongong and Kiama way,' she clarified. 'The beaches an hour or two south of Sydney.'

He'd swum those beaches once upon a time. A lifetime ago. A life that felt as if it had belonged to somebody else.

He shook the thought off. 'The beaches here are similar to the ones you'd be used to back home.' Tesoura's beaches were probably safer than most.

'Thank you.' The smile she flashed him pierced beneath his guard, making that damn ache start up in the centre of him again. Her smile faded, though, when he didn't smile back, and he did his damnedest to not feel guilty about it. 'I'm sorry, I should've asked your permission before using your computer.'

Which raised another question. 'I don't want

you touching any of the equipment in this room, Ms Hartley.'

She nodded and apologised again, hesitated and then said, 'I guess there's no chance of you calling me Imogen, is there?'

'None whatsoever.' He did his best not to feel guilty about that either. 'Didn't you bring a laptop or tablet to the island?'

For some reason that made her laugh. 'Ah, but, you see, I haven't been given the keys to the kingdom.'

What on earth was she talking about?

'The Wi-Fi password,' she clarified.

Why on earth not?

'Apparently I don't have the right security clearance.' Her lips twitched irresistibly. 'It must be above my pay grade.'

She quoted that last sentence as if it was a line from a movie, but he wasn't familiar with it. Then again, he couldn't remember the last time he'd watched a movie.

He pushed that thought aside. Why on earth hadn't Katherine given her niece the password?

None of his business. He knew Katherine was keeping secrets from her family, but he had no intention of getting involved. Without a word, he wrote the login details down and pushed them across to her.

She glanced at them and her eyes started to dance. 'Does that mean I just got a promotion?'

He resisted the urge to smile back. 'It now means you can log onto the Internet using your own devices rather than mine, Ms Hartley.'

The smile dropped from her lips. Again. Banter with the boss wasn't going to happen and the sooner she understood that, the better.

Something rebellious and resentful at the strictures he'd placed upon himself prickled through him, but he squashed it. It was for the best.

She shifted from one leg to the other. 'Look, I wanted to apologise again about earlier. I—'

'It's all forgotten, Ms Hartley.'

'But—'

'I'd appreciate it if you'd close the door on your way out.'

He turned back to his computer and opened a fresh spreadsheet. She stood there frozen for a moment, and then shook herself. 'Yes, of course, sir.'

And if her *sir* held an edge of sarcasm, he didn't bother calling her on it. He wasn't interested in winning any Best Boss of the Year awards. Imogen was only here temporarily while Katherine sorted a few things out. She'd be gone again in a flash. And peace would reign once more.

The moment she left he closed the spreadsheet. He'd only opened it to look busy and get Imogen to leave his office. Ms Hartley, he corrected. *Not Imogen.* He checked his Internet browsing history more thoroughly.

She'd started precisely one search. That was it. She'd wanted to know the surf conditions. As she'd said. She wasn't a journalist. She hadn't lied.

Good. He hadn't relished the thought of telling Katherine her niece was a thief, liar or cheat. He eased back in his seat, glad that the open friendliness of Imogen's face wasn't a front for deception. He was glad his instincts hadn't let him down.

You could've made an effort to be a little friendlier.

He squashed the notion dead. No, he couldn't. It started with a couple of shared jokes, and evolved to shared confidences, and before you knew it a friendship had formed—a friendship you'd started to rely on. But when it all went to hell in a handbasket you found out that you couldn't rely on anyone. Not your friends, not your girlfriend and sure as hell not your family. He wasn't walking that road again.

It was easier to not start anything at all. He'd learned to rely on nothing beyond his own resources. It'd worked perfectly for the past two years, and if it wasn't broken…

A sudden image of Imogen's face—the fear in her eyes as she'd edged away from him—speared into his gut, making a cold sweat break out on his nape. Who was he kidding? *He* was broken.

And a man like him needed to stay away from a woman like Imogen Hartley.

Shooting to his feet, he strode to the window, his lip curling at the tropical perfection that greeted him. He should've chosen the site of his exile with more care—picked some forlorn and windswept scrap of rock off the coast of Scotland or…or Norway. All grey forbidding stone, frozen winds and stunted trees.

Two years ago, though, all he'd cared about was getting as far from Australia as he could, as quickly as he could.

He wheeled away from the window. He'd never cared that the island was beautiful before, so why wish himself away from it now? He should never have cut his run short—that was the problem. Running and swimming kept the demons at bay.

He should've stuck to his routine. And a hard forty minutes' worth of laps would rectify that.

He flung the door of his office open at the exact same moment the front doorbell sounded. He blinked. He hadn't known that the doorbell even worked. It hadn't rung in the two years he'd been in residence. All deliveries—food and office supplies, the mail—were delivered to the back door and Katherine. The villa was huge and sprawling, and the back entrance was closer to the jetty, which suited everyone. Nobody visited Tesoura. *Nobody.*

He'd bet his life it was Imogen Hartley. She'd probably rung it for a lark. She was exactly the kind of person who'd do that—just for the fun of it, to see if it worked. He waited for her to pop her head into the room and apologise. She'd probably feed him some story about polishing it or some such nonsense. He'd even be gracious about it.

Imogen came rushing through from the direction of the kitchen. 'Was that the—?'

The doorbell rang again.

'—the doorbell?' she finished.

He gestured towards the front entrance, his gut clenching. 'I'd appreciate it if you'd answer it, Ms Hartley.'

Those vivacious eyes danced as she started for the door. 'Butler is definitely a promotion.'

Even if he hadn't put his 'no smiling' rule into place, he couldn't have smiled now if he'd wanted to. Somebody ringing the front doorbell here on his island miles from civilisation could only mean one thing—trouble. 'If it's the press...' he managed before she disappeared into the front hall.

She swung around. 'Short shrift?'

'Please.'

She gave him a thumbs-up in reply before disappearing, and despite himself a smile tugged at his lips. The woman was irrepressible.

He stayed out of sight but moved closer so he could listen.

'I understand this is the residence of Jasper Coleman,' a pleasantly cultured male voice said.

'May I ask who's calling, please?'

He couldn't fault Imogen's tone—courteous, professional...unflappable.

'I have a delivery for him.' There was a series of dull thuds, as if things were being dropped to the ground, and then a softer click and scrape. 'Don't worry, he doesn't have to sign for it.'

Unflappable disappeared when Imogen yelped, 'That's a baby!'

What?

'Hey, wait! You can't just leave a baby here.'

'Those were my instructions, miss.' The voice started to recede. 'Just following orders.'

Jasper shot out from his hiding place in time to see his *butler* accost a man almost twice her size and pull him to a halt. 'What is wrong with you? You can't just go around dumping unknown babies on people's doorsteps.'

'The baby is neither unknown nor am I dumping him. I was hired to escort the baby to Mr Coleman. And I'm rather pleased to have managed it before his next feed is due. As far as I'm concerned, my job here is done.'

Ice trickled down Jasper's spine. Ignoring it—and the baby capsule sitting on his doorstep—he forced himself forward. 'There has to be some mistake.'

'No mistake,' the man said, turning towards Jasper. 'Not if you're Jasper Coleman.'

Imogen released the man's arm and stepped back to let Jasper deal with the situation, but she didn't disappear back inside the house and he didn't know whether to be glad of her silent support or not.

'You *are* Jasper Coleman, right?'

He wanted to lie, but there was a baby involved. 'Yes.'

'Then there's no mistake.'

His gut clenched. There was only one person who would send him a baby, but… It was impossible! She'd said she hated him. She'd said he'd ruined her life.

The man gestured to the baby capsule. 'Mr Coleman, meet your nephew.'

On cue, the baby opened his eyes and gave a loud wail.

Jasper couldn't move. 'What's he doing here?'

'Your sister hired me to escort the baby here from Australia.' He pulled a card from his pocket and handed it across. 'Belforte's Executive Nanny Service, sir.'

'You're a nanny?'

'One of the best. If you check with the office, you'll see that everything is in order. I believe you'll find a letter from your sister in one of the bags. I expect it'll explain everything.' And then he frowned as if suddenly recalling something. 'Mrs Graham did say that if I saw you to say the word *Jupiter*. She said you'd know what that meant.'

His gut twisted. Jupiter had been their password as kids.

The baby's cries grew louder and more per-sistent.

He was aware of Imogen glancing from him to the nanny and back again, but he couldn't meet her eye. He couldn't move.

'You'll have to excuse me. I'm expected in Rio for my next assignment by nightfall. Have a nice day.' And then he turned and strode away, evi-dently washing his hands of them all. And who could blame him? It wasn't *his* baby.

It didn't stop Jasper from wanting to tackle him to the ground and force him to take the baby back. *Damn!* What game was Emily playing now? He swallowed down his panic and chan-nelled the coldness he'd spent the last two years perfecting. He would find a way to deal with this and—

Imogen pushed past him to sweep the crying baby up into her arms and cuddle him. 'Hey there, little dude, what's all this fuss about? You feeling a bit discombobulated? I don't blame you.'

The baby batted his face into her shoulder a couple of times, rubbed a fist across his eyes, while Imogen cooed nonsense, and then he fi-nally looked up at her. She sent him a big smile before blowing a raspberry into his hand. To

Jasper's utter astonishment the baby not only stopped crying but smiled back, as if Imogen was the best thing he'd seen all day.

And Imogen Hartley visibly melted.

Right, she'd said she'd wanted a promotion. He wondered how she'd feel about the position of nanny?

CHAPTER TWO

IMOGEN BOUNCED THE baby on her hip and winced at Jasper's white-faced shock. A baby turning up on his doorstep was obviously the last thing he'd expected. Cool eyes darkened and a bitter resignation twisted his lips, making her heart thump. She fought an urge to go over and put her arm around him, to try and comfort him the way she did the baby.

But why should he need comforting?

She moistened her lips. 'This is your nephew?'

He nodded.

She waited, but he didn't offer anything else. 'What's his name?'

'George.'

It was too hard to look at Jasper, so she smiled at George instead. 'Hello, gorgy Georgie!'

Jasper swore. Not particularly badly, but with a venom that made both her and the baby jump. *Okay.* So he *really* hadn't expected the arrival of this baby. And he was *really* unhappy about it.

But little George stared at his uncle with wide fear-filled eyes and looked as if he was about to start crying again. So she bounced him gently and started singing, 'I'm a little teapot.'

The baby turned to her again and his face broke out into a big smile. He waved his hands and made lots of inarticulate noises. What an adorable bundle of chubby-cheeked cuteness!

'Hey, you going to be a singer, little guy?' She glanced at his uncle. 'How old is he?'

'Nine months.' Jasper stared at her oddly. 'You're very good with him.'

'Back in the real world I'm Auntie Immy to four of the cutest babies on the planet.'

'I thought you were an only child?'

Ah, so Aunt Katherine had told him a little about her, then. What other confidences had she shared? 'An honorary aunt.' She stuck her nose in the air. 'Which everyone knows is the best kind.'

He stared at her for a moment before one side of his mouth hooked up. Her heart stilled mid-beat, before pounding again with ferocious abandon. That half smile transformed him completely— the stern mouth curved with a sensual lilt that chased away some of the shadows in his eyes. It made her think of summer and fun and…ice cream. She fought to catch her breath. From the first moment she'd clapped eyes on Jasper, everything about him had screamed undeniable maleness. But now he was also unmistakably gorgeous.

He sobered, the frown returning to his face, and she dragged her gaze away. Dear God, please don't let him have misconstrued her scrutiny.

She scuffed a toe against the ground and tried to hide a grimace. What was there to misconstrue? She'd been ogling him, which was seriously poor form. But it didn't mean she had designs on him or anything, and—

'Are you feeling all right, Ms Hartley?'

She realised she'd scrunched her face up, and immediately set about un-scrunching it. 'Thought I was going to sneeze.'

He raised an eyebrow.

'It didn't seem like a good idea with an armful of baby,' she improvised. She wanted—no, needed—him to stop looking at her in that way. She gestured to the series of bags that George's minder had dropped to the doorstep. 'I guess we should get these out of the sun.' Without another word, she grabbed the baby capsule at her feet and strode through into Jasper's impeccable living room.

She grinned at the baby. 'Oh, you're going to mess this up perfectly, master George.'

'How is he going to mess it up?' Jasper said, coming in behind her. 'Is he old enough to walk?'

'Unlikely, though he might be crawling. Hey, little dude, are you speeding around yet?' She sent Jasper a grin. 'I'll show you what I mean.' She went to hand him George, but he took a physical step away, a look of horror speeding across his face.

Whoa.

She gulped down the words that pressed against the back of her throat. There was something going on here that she didn't understand, and the last thing little George needed was for her to make it worse. So she instead pointed to the bags. 'In one of those there are bound to be some toys and a baby blanket.'

Without another word, he started rummaging and eventually found what she'd asked for. Handing her the blanket, he held a toy out in each hand—a plastic set of keys on a key ring in primary colours, and a plush bunny rabbit with long ears. With a squeal, George reached for the keys.

Very carefully, Jasper handed them over.

Imogen spread the blanket on the living room's

thick designer rug and then upended the rest of the contents of the bag across it.

'What the—?'

Setting a boomerang pillow in the middle of it all, she very gently settled George into its curve before pulling the toys closer. He threw the keys, waved his arms about and started making *broom-broom* noises.

She reached for a toy car. 'Is this what you're after, little guy?'

He grabbed it, immediately shoving one corner of it in his mouth.

Imogen rose and gestured to the baby, the rug, and the assortment of toys. 'Hey, presto, your living room isn't quite so immaculate.'

He eyed her carefully. 'You sound as if you approve of the change.'

'It's very hard to disapprove of babies, Uncle Jasp—Mr Coleman,' she amended in a rush, heat flushing through her cheeks.

What on earth…? Just because there was a baby in the house didn't mean she could dispense with normal boss-employee formality.

He let her near slip pass, just continued to stare at her. Um…?

Oh! She was supposed to be working. He was probably wondering what on earth she was still doing here lingering in his living room as if she owned it. Swallowing, she backed up a step. 'I guess I better get back to work and—'

'No!'

She halted, mentally tutoring herself on the appropriate levels of deference due to an employer. 'Sir?'

'I have a proposition to put to you, Ms Hartley.'

She glanced at baby George, who was happily banging a plastic hammer against his foot, and she started to laugh. 'I just bet you do.'

Damn! Couldn't she maintain a semblance of polite dutifulness for even thirty seconds?

He eyed the baby and then her. 'You did say you wanted a promotion.'

She'd been joking! And while it hadn't been a joke that'd made him laugh, or even smile, she knew he hadn't taken her seriously. 'Is nanny a promotion?'

'Absolutely. It comes with a higher pay grade, for a start.'

She didn't care about the money. The money wasn't the reason she was here.

'With all the associated security clearances.'

Had he just made a joke? She grinned—partly in shock but mostly in delight. 'Now that *is* an attractive fringe benefit.'

'Is that a yes, then?'

She glanced at the baby. It'd be way more fun to look after George, but it wasn't why she was here.

'You're hesitating. May I ask why?' He gestured to the baby. 'You seem a natural. While I understand there may be some allure to dancing with vacuum cleaners, you did seem to enjoy singing nursery rhymes too.'

She'd definitely rather look after George than dust and vacuum, but she'd promised her mother she'd find out what was troubling Aunt Katherine. Looking after a baby 24/7 could put a serious dent in the amount of time she could give to that.

'Ms Hartley?'

'Mr Coleman, I have a feeling that your idea of what being a nanny involves and my idea of the same are worlds apart.'

He blinked.

She nodded at the letter he held—the letter from his sister that he still hadn't opened. 'You don't know how long George is here for. You don't know what his mother's wishes are and—'

'How will our ideas about a nanny's duties differ?'

She eyed him uncertainly. 'I think you'll expect me to be on duty twenty-four hours a day, seven days a week. And I'm sorry, but I'm not interested in working those kinds of hours. That's not the reason I came to Tesoura. I'm here to spend some time with my aunt. And in my free time I plan to lap up all of the tropical gorgeousness that I can.' Until she returned home, and her real life started. A thrill rippled through her at the thought…along with a growing thread of fear. 'The former is going to prove difficult and the latter impossible with a baby in tow.'

He tapped a finger against his lips. 'Asking you to work those hours would be completely unreasonable.' He said the words with such a deep regret that in other circumstances she might've laughed.

She didn't laugh. She edged towards the door before she weakened and did what he wanted— became a full-time carer to that gorgeous bundle of baby.

'Where are you going?'

His sharp tone pulled her to a halt. 'To go and perform the duties you're currently paying me for.'

'You can't leave me alone with the baby.' Panic rippled across his face. *'Please.'*

That *please* caught at her, tugged on all of

her sympathies and completely baffled her. 'Why not?'

'I don't know a single thing about babies.'

George had been staring at them as if aware of the tension that had started to zing through the air, and he promptly burst into tears. She didn't blame him. She swooped down and lifted him in her arms, patting his back as he snuffled against her neck. 'Well, lesson number one is to not yell around them. It upsets them.'

Aunt Katherine came into the room with her brisk step. 'Goodness, I thought I heard a baby. So the cot and pram that were just delivered weren't mistakes, then?'

Jasper gave a curt shake of his head and gestured towards George. 'Emily's baby.'

Her aunt's eyes widened. 'Well, now, that's a turn up for the books.' She moved across and clasped one of George's hands. 'Hello, little man, it's nice to meet you. I knew your mummy, back in the days before you were born.' She glanced back at Jasper. 'Poor little tyke looks tired. How long is he here for?'

He shook his head. 'I don't know.'

Imogen refrained from pointing out that if he read his sister's letter, they might get an answer to that particular question.

Katherine pursed her lips. 'Right.'

Imogen glanced from one to the other, trying to make their relationship out. Katherine had been on the island for the past two years. Before that she'd worked for the Coleman family for seventeen years. Were they friends? She bit her lip. Were they lovers? The question disturbed her, though she couldn't have said why. At forty-nine Katherine was still young, and she was certainly attractive. While Jasper would be what—mid-thirties? It didn't seem outside the realm of possibility.

Her aunt was keeping secrets. Every instinct Imogen had told her that. Was Jasper one of those secrets?

If he were either a friend or a lover, though, he'd have given Katherine the week's leave she'd requested at Christmastime.

Her aunt's laughter hurtled her back. 'Don't look at me like that, Jasper, because the answer is a big fat no. If I'd wanted to look after a baby, I'd have had one of my own.'

That made Imogen smile. Katherine didn't have a maternal bone in her body.

'But—'

'No buts,' Katherine said without ceremony. She glanced at Imogen and then Jasper again, and her eyes started to gleam. 'I'll let you continue your negotiations with Imogen, shall I?'

'What negotiations?' he grumbled. 'She's as hard-headed as you.'

Imogen surveyed her perplexing boss. For someone who'd been shocked into white-faced silence at the arrival of the baby, he seemed to have taken it into his stride now, seemed almost...resigned. Why—if he didn't want the baby here—wasn't he making arrangements to send the child back?

Katherine turned and patted Imogen's arm. In a low voice she said, 'Get him to help with the baby,' before disappearing into the kitchen.

If she did what her aunt asked, would Katherine stop avoiding her and tell her what was wrong?

'What did your aunt just say to you?'

She did her best to smooth out her face. 'Only that lunch is ready.'

His eyes narrowed, but he didn't call her on the lie. She pulled in a breath. 'Mr Coleman, I think between the three of us we can work something out.'

He widened his stance. 'You heard your aunt— she'll have nothing to do with him.'

'She won't change dirty nappies or bathe

George. But she'll give him a bottle and be happy to keep an eye on him when he's napping.'

'There's one other thing you need to take into consideration, Ms Hartley, and that's the fact that I'm *not* looking after that baby.'

'Mr Coleman,' she said very gently, 'that's not my problem. It's yours.'

He knew he was being unreasonable—not to mention irrational—but he could barely check the panic coursing through him. It'd smashed through the walls he'd put up to contain it, and while part of him knew the panic was illogical, another part understood all too clearly that he had every reason to fear the consequences of his nephew's visit.

Aaron wanted revenge, and Jasper didn't doubt that his brother-in-law would use George as a weapon—to hurt him or extort money from him. That was the best-case scenario he could come up with—that Aaron wanted money. And Jasper would give money—a lot of money—to keep this child safe.

But he'd learned to not rely on best-case scenarios. With his luck in another day or two police would show up and arrest him for allegedly kidnapping the baby. And then he'd be charged, and there'd be court proceedings…again. The thought had exhaustion sweeping through him.

Ms Hartley was right, though. This wasn't her problem. It was his. He dropped to the edge of the nearest sofa.

Focus.

Fact number one: the baby was here now, and arrangements needed to be made for his care. Fact number two: he didn't want the press getting wind of this—whatever *this* was. Instinct warned him it'd be wiser to scotch any rumours before they started. He had to keep this as quiet as possible, which meant the fewer people who knew, the better. *Those* were the important facts for the moment. He could worry about the rest later.

'Can…can you just stay there with the baby while I make a phone call?'

She frowned but nodded. Not giving her a chance to change her mind, he grabbed his phone and speed-dialled his assistant in Sydney. He needed information. 'Evan, my sister has just had a nanny service deliver her baby to my house without warning.'

Two seconds of silence greeted him before Evan said, 'What do you need me to do?'

'Can you find out what Emily and Aaron's movements are at the moment? *Discreetly*.'

'I'll be in touch as soon as I find anything out.'

'The sooner the better, please.'

He tossed his phone to the coffee table and scratched a hand across his head. It was entirely unreasonable to ask Imogen to be on call with the baby all the hours of the day and night. It contravened every workplace agreement he subscribed to. It was unethical. He'd taken great pains to ensure his company's workplace practices were above reproach. It was especially important now to continue in the same vein.

Besides, neither Katherine nor Imogen were the kind of women to be browbeaten by a domineering boss. Not that he was domineering, but he wouldn't be able to cajole either one of them into doing something they didn't want to do. There was a part of him that was glad about that. It indicated that they had integrity. It was important right now to surround himself with people of integrity.

The sofa dipped a little as Imogen sat beside him. 'I want to pat your back much the same way as I am little George's at the moment.'

He met warm brown eyes flecked with green

and filled with sympathy. He straightened. 'Please don't.' The thought of her touching him…

He cut the thought off.

George had nestled his head in against her shoulder and noisily sucked a dummy, while she rubbed slow, soothing circles to his back—lulling and hypnotic. It took a force of will to lift his gaze back to her face. Up this close he could see the light spattering of freckles across her nose.

'Of course I'd not do anything so forward. But it's obvious your nephew's arrival has come as something of a shock.'

Understatement of the century.

'I think I should leave you in peace for the next hour or so to read your sister's letter, and to take stock of the situation. I'll keep this little guy with me for the present.'

That was kind, but…

'Wait,' he said as she started to rise.

She subsided back to the sofa. He let out a low breath. He wasn't ready to read Emily's letter yet. He wasn't sure he'd be able to believe a single word it said. 'You honestly believe that between the three of us, we'd be able to look after the baby?'

'Yes.'

'How would you see that working?'

She shrugged, and her chin-length hair—a mass of dark curls—bounced and bobbed. 'A little bit of give and take on all sides, I expect. Though probably mostly from yours.'

He didn't like the sound of that much. Still… needs must. 'In what way?'

'You'd need to cut down on some of your working hours to help out with George.'

He'd expected that.

'Mind you, that could be a good thing. Seems to me you work too hard anyway.'

The moment the words left her mouth, she shot back in her seat. 'I can't believe I just said that. It was way too personal and completely out of line. I'm sorry.'

She was holding his nephew, rubbing his back—and she spoke the truth—so he let it pass. He worked long hours because, like the swimming and the running, it helped to keep the demons at bay. Keeping busy kept him sane. For the duration of the baby's stay he'd simply be busy helping look after him instead of wrestling with complicated computer code. It wouldn't have to be any different from his current routine.

'And while George is here, you might need to…'

He raised an eyebrow.

'Lower your standards of cleanliness.'

He blinked.

'If I'm looking after George for part of the day and night, I'm not going to have the same amount of time to devote to cleaning your house.'

'That's fine with me.' In fact, it was more than fine. 'Ms Hartley, you've vacuumed and dusted these rooms every day since you arrived. Now far be it from me to question your work practices—I've never been to housekeeping school, so I don't know what the norm is—but don't you think vacuuming every day is overkill? I'm tidy in my habits, don't tramp mud into the house on a regular basis, and don't have children or dogs—' He broke off to glance at the baby in her arms. 'I don't *usually* have children or dogs to stay.'

'But Aunt Katherine said you had the highest expectations when it came to—' She broke off, biting her lip.

What on earth had Katherine been telling her niece?

He pushed the thought away. He had more pressing concerns at the moment. 'I'm happy to relax the current cleaning standards.' He pulled in a breath. 'There's just one other little problem in your proposed plan.'

'Which is?'

His stomach churned. 'I don't have the first idea about babies. I don't have a clue how to feed them or what to feed them or how to prepare whatever it is that you do feed them. I've never changed a nappy. The thought doesn't fill me with a great deal of enthusiasm, admittedly, but evidently it's a chore I'm not going to be able to avoid. And precisely how do you bathe a baby without drowning it? Don't they get slippery and hard to hold? That sounds like a disaster waiting to happen, if you ask me.'

She smiled, the green sparks in her eyes dancing, and the impact of it hit him in the middle of his chest, making his heart thump.

'I can teach you all of those things easy-peasy. But there are a couple of other things you'll need to learn too, like cuddling and playing. Both are vital to a baby's development.'

Before he knew what she was about, she'd leaned forward and set the baby on his lap, and he wanted to yell at her to take him back. But recalled, just in time, that he wasn't supposed to yell around the baby. He wanted to shoot to his feet and race away. But he couldn't because he had *a lap full of baby.*

He wasn't sure how the kid would've reacted if he'd been fully awake—with a loud verbal protest he suspected—but, drowsy as he was, he merely nestled in against Jasper's chest. The warm weight made his heart thud, made him wonder when was the last time he'd actually touched someone? *Hell!* He—

'Stop frowning,' she chided gently from where she'd moved to kneel in front of him, adjusting his arm so it went fully around the baby with his hand resting on the child's tummy. 'We don't want George glancing up and being frightened out of his wits by the scary man glaring at him.'

The thought that he could so easily frighten his nephew sickened him.

'I mean, that's hard enough for a grown-up to deal with.'

Her voice held laughter, but that didn't stop his gaze from spearing hers. 'I'm sorry I scared you earlier. I really didn't mean to.'

'I know that now. I overreacted, but—'

He looped his fingers around her wrist. 'Never apologise for trusting your instincts and being cautious. It's better to feel a little foolish than it is to get hurt—every single time. No exceptions.'

She stared at his hand on her wrist and nodded. She'd gone very still. Had he frightened her again? He didn't hold her tightly. She could move away at any time… Her tongue snaked out to moisten her lips and something hot and sweet licked along his veins.

He let her go in an instant.

She eased away, colour high on her cheekbones. 'Do you mind if I check the bags?' She gestured to the muddle of bags that apparently came with a baby.

'By all means. Are you looking for anything in particular?' If she took the baby back he'd look for her.

'George's schedule.' He must've looked clueless because she added, 'Feed times, nap times… those sorts of things.'

He tried to do what she was doing—focussing on the situation with the baby rather than that moment of…

He didn't know what to call it. A moment of awareness that had taken them both off guard. He pulled in a breath and counted to ten.

Emotions were running high, that was all. He was holding his nephew, for heaven's sake. A nephew he'd thought he'd never get to meet, let alone hold. It was making him hyper-aware of everything. What he didn't need to notice at the moment, however, was the silkiness of his housemaid's skin or the shininess of her hair. He gritted his teeth. Or the beguiling shape of her mouth.

He forced his gaze to the baby who, with half-closed eyes, continued to suck on his dummy with a kind of focussed fierceness. His chest clenched. What kind of unfairness or…or whim had turned this little guy's life upside down? The innate fragility and helplessness of the baby, the sense of responsibility that suddenly weighed down on him, had his former panic stirring. How could he do this? How—?

'I didn't go to housekeeping school either,' Imogen said out of the blue. 'Just so you know. In case you hadn't worked that out for yourself yet.'

She sat cross-legged on the rug, going methodically through each of the bags. And she was telling him this because…?

'I wouldn't want you accusing me at some distant point in the future of being here under false pretences.'

He recalled how she'd puffed up earlier when she'd thought he'd been slighting her intelligence. Did she feel lesser because she'd not been to the right school or wasn't properly qualified or something? Focussing on her issues was certainly better than focussing on the baby he held. 'It doesn't necessarily follow that you're not a hard worker, though, right?'

'Exactly!' Her smile was so bright it could blind a man. He blinked but he couldn't look away. And then she grimaced. 'I don't have the subservient thing down pat yet, though.'

His lips twitched. 'I hadn't noticed.'

'Ooh.' Her grin widened and she pointed a finger at him. 'You just made a joke.'

He ignored that. Making jokes at the moment was no doubt highly inappropriate. For heaven's sake, *he was holding a baby.* 'Ms Hartley, let me put your mind at rest. I trust Katherine's judgement.'

'Even though I'm family?'

She's a bit flighty and irresponsible.

He didn't see any evidence of that. 'Even then,' he said. He spoke without hesitation. He'd trust Kate with his life. He knew she was keeping secrets from her family, but they were harmless enough. He couldn't blame her for protecting her privacy when he'd all but exiled himself to a remote island.

She's a bit flighty and irresponsible. He suspected Kate had lied about that to put an invisible wedge between him and her niece. He didn't blame her for wanting to protect Imogen from a man like him. He didn't consider himself a good prospect either.

Imogen halted from her rifling of bags. 'I want to apologise for my rudeness earlier.'

She'd been rude?

'I shouldn't have jumped on you like that for calling me stupid.'

'I did *not* call you stupid.'

'You know what I mean.'

She'd only been responding to his rudeness. 'I shouldn't have been so short with you.'

One shoulder lifted. 'I'm a bit sensitive on the subject, and I shouldn't have flared up like that.'

He stared at her for a moment. 'Why are you sensitive?'

She ducked her head. 'It doesn't matter.'

He had a feeling it mattered a great deal.

He wasn't sure what she saw in his face when she glanced back up, but whatever it was had her heaving out a sigh. 'I don't think I'm stupid, Mr Coleman. I know I'm not. I'm just a bit sensitive about it at the moment because last week, before I came here, I ran into an old boyfriend— my high-school sweetheart.'

From the look on her face he'd been anything but a sweetheart.

'When he found out I had no plans to go to university—like him—he told me I was...'

'Stupid?'

'I believe the words he used were *uneducated yokel*.' She shrugged. 'Naturally I kicked his sorry butt to the kerb.'

'*Smart* move.'

'But, you know, that was seven years ago, and people grow up, so when I saw him last week I said hello.' Her lips thinned. 'That wasn't quite so smart.'

A hard ball settled in the pit of his stomach. 'He called you stupid again?'

'Implied it.'

What a jerk! 'Why?'

She shook her head. 'It doesn't matter.'

He didn't believe that for a moment.

'I'm *not* stupid and what I'm doing with my life *isn't* stupid or risky. It's just...his voice has wormed its way inside my head, and I haven't been able to shake it. I'm sorry you were the one who had his head snapped off, though.'

'I have broad shoulders.' He shrugged. 'And if you want the truth, I came back early from my run to apologise for being so grumpy.'

She folded her arms and stared at him. 'You know what? You're not the slightest bit difficult or temperamental.'

What on earth had made her think he was?

Katherine. The answer came to him swiftly. Katherine didn't want him messing with her niece, and he had no intention of giving the older woman cause for concern. He might not be difficult and temperamental, and Imogen might not be flighty and irresponsible. But their lives were poles apart. And he had every intention of keeping them that way.

CHAPTER THREE

THE MYRIAD EXPRESSIONS that chased themselves across Jasper's face pierced Imogen with unexpected force. Her heart beat too hard—a pounding that rose into her throat and made it ache.

She didn't bother tempering the sympathy that raged through her. She doubted she'd be successful even if she tried. He'd stared at his nephew with a mixture of such shock and wonder, pain and hope and desolation, that it had almost overwhelmed her. She understood the shock and the hope, but not the pain and desolation. And certainly not the fear.

A bit of panic—yes.

Worry and anxiety—absolutely.

But not that bone-crushing fear that had seemed to be directed both inwards and outwards at the same time. She'd been desperate to rid him of that expression, so she'd overshared. Again.

But that was better than staring at his awful

expression and doing nothing about it. The lines fanning out from serious grey eyes were still strained and the grooves bracketing his mouth were still deep, but he no longer looked so worn or overwhelmed.

The grey of those eyes was quite extraordinary. She'd never seen eyes like them—silver in some lights, they held a hint of blue in others, but could deepen to charcoal and concentrate so intensely you felt spotlighted...and seen, *really* seen.

'All right, Ms Hartley, let's try your suggestion and see if, between the three of us, we can manage. I'll increase your and your aunt's salaries for as long as the baby is here and—'

'Oh, that's not necessary.' He was already paying her a generous salary.

'You'll both be taking on extra duties and I have no intention of taking advantage of your good natures. We'll do things by the book. You'll be compensated accordingly.'

He wanted this to be a work arrangement, rather than a favour between friends. Which suited her fine because they *weren't* friends. She recalled the awful expression that had overtaken his face and couldn't help thinking that the one thing Jasper Coleman could do with at the moment, though, was a friend.

She glanced at George, noting the way he worried at his dummy. 'He's due for his bottle.'

'You'd better take him, then.'

She suspected that if he'd had more confidence in handling babies, he'd have simply handed him over, and she'd have had no choice but to take him. As it was, he stared at her expectantly, evidently expecting her to obey him immediately, and she had to fight her instant response to do exactly that. 'I will, but first I want to make a request.'

His brows rose. Yep. He'd expected her to jump to do his bidding immediately.

It's what he's paying you for, Imogen.

'Is it possible for us to drop the Mr Coleman and Ms Hartley and call each other by our first names? I know I'm only a housemaid with a promotion to a third of a nanny's position while you're a genius billionaire, but I can promise you I won't forget the distinction. The thing is, I've never worked in an environment that maintained such formalities, and I just know I'm going to slip up and call you Uncle Jasper to little George here at some point. "Go to Uncle Jasper, Georgie,"' she sing-songed to demonstrate what she meant. 'It'd be really nice if we could eliminate that worry right now.'

She couldn't work out if he was trying not to smile or trying not to frown.

'You don't look particularly worried, Ms Hartley.'

Was that a no? 'I can assure you that I'm shaking on the inside.'

She bit back a sigh when he didn't smile. Mind you, he didn't frown either. She tried again. 'You and my aunt call each other by your first names. I promise not to take any liberties just because we move to a more informal mode of address.'

He stared at her for several long seconds. 'Are you familiar with the movie *The Sound of Music*?' he finally asked.

'Intimately.' It was one of her favourites. 'An oldie but a goodie.'

'I'm vividly reminded of the moment in the film where the captain asks Maria if she was this much trouble at the abbey.'

A bark of laughter shot out of her. 'And she answers, "Oh, much more, sir."' She glanced at the baby in his arms. 'I have to say I'm *very* glad you weren't just landed with seven children.'

As if they couldn't help it, his lips lifted. Her pulse shimmied and all the fine hairs on her arms Mexican-waved.

'Very well, Imogen, first names it is. Perhaps now you'll be good enough to take the baby?'

He angled the side holding the baby towards her, and she moved closer, ordering various parts of herself to stop tripping the light fantastic. 'Hey there, beautiful boy.' George came willingly, but not before Imogen had sucked in a deep breath of Jasper-scented air.

He smelled of the sea and the sweat from his run and something darker and spicier, like cardamom. The smell of sweat especially should've had her nose wrinkling, but it didn't. She edged away before she could be tempted to drag in another appreciative lungful.

His sister's letter still sat unopened on the arm of the sofa. Why hadn't he torn it open and devoured its contents yet? She adjusted her weight from one leg to the other. 'May I make a suggestion?'

'You may.'

'I think you should read your sister's letter. And before you accuse me of taking those liberties that I promised I wouldn't, I want to assure you that I'm not trying to pry. Your family's concerns are none of my business. But we need to know if George has any medical issues or medications that he's taking or any allergies.' She lifted the schedule of feeding and nap times she'd found in the same bag that held some ready-made bottles of formula. 'None of those things are mentioned here, which probably means that there's nothing to worry about,' she added quickly at the look of absolute horror that passed across his face. 'But with knowledge being power and all that,' she finished on a weak shrug.

Surely no mother would send her baby somewhere so remote—so far from medical facilities—if he had a known medical condition like asthma, though. At least…not a good mother. She glanced at the baby in her arms. Sympathy, compassion, pity and foreboding all churned in her stomach. Why on earth would *any* mother send her child away? Was Jasper's sister a good mother or—?

'Why are you frowning, Imogen?'

She started. 'Oh, I…'

'I'd rather know. Especially if it pertains to the baby.'

He hadn't called *the baby* by his name yet—not once. What was that about? Though she wasn't silly enough to ask that question either…yet.

'Your sister would tell us if there were any issues we should be aware of where George is concerned, right?'

She waited for him to reassure her. He didn't. His shoulders didn't slump, but it felt as if they ought to, that they were only remaining in place due to some superhuman effort on his behalf. 'I don't know. My sister and I have been estranged for the last two years.'

Why?

She didn't ask that either. He didn't look as if he had the heart for it. She focussed her attention on the baby instead. 'How about we make a pact, little George? While you're here you're only going to get all good things. What do you say to that?'

He spat out his dummy and gave a grumpy grunt that reminded her so much of his uncle it made her laugh. 'I'm glad we got that sorted. It's going to be nothing but sun and fun and kisses and cuddles and good times, right?'

He nodded, copying her, and he looked so darn cute she found herself automatically swinging back to Jasper to share the moment. She found him staring at them with an arrested expression on his face, and it had her smile freezing and all of that shimmying and Mexican-waving happening all over again.

She had to get that under control because *that* wasn't going to happen here. Instinct told her that if Jasper thought for a single solitary second that she was attracted to him, he'd boot her off his island faster than she could sew a side seam. She couldn't let *that* happen until she'd found out what was troubling Katherine.

She swung away, grabbing up the bag with the bottles and formula. 'I'll go and warm up George's bottle.' And she didn't glance back once as she marched from the room. She kept her gaze trained on little George, who clapped his hands together and chanted, 'Yum, yum, yum.'

Both she and George were chanting, 'Yum, yum, yum,' as they entered the kitchen.

Katherine glanced up from where she sat at the table with a glass of iced tea. 'I expect you're both hungry.'

'Ravenous,' she agreed, pulling a bottle from the bag and setting it in the microwave.

'Here, give him to me,' Katherine said when the bottle was ready. 'I'll feed him while you eat your sandwich.'

Imogen did as she bid. Maybe little George here could be the icebreaker she needed with her aunt?

They both watched as the baby fed greedily, his eyes closing in bliss. 'Eat up, Immy, because you're burping him. I don't do vomit. Or nappies.'

Imogen grabbed her sandwich from the fridge—chicken salad, her favourite—and started eating too.

'What's been decided?'

'I told Jasper that between the three of us, we'd be able to manage. I thought he was going to explode.' She winked. 'But he eventually saw the wisdom of my suggestion.'

Katherine snorted.

'We're both being paid higher duties for the duration of George's visit. And before you ask, I've no idea how long that's likely to be.'

Katherine raised an eyebrow. 'He's really agreed to help with the baby?'

She bit into her sandwich and nodded. 'He wasn't what you'd call enthusiastic—' *resigned* might be the appropriate term '—but he agreed to let me teach him what he needs to know.'

'Good for you.'

He hadn't been the least bit unreasonable or temperamental. She glanced at her aunt before feigning interest in her sandwich again. 'While I'm more than happy to pull my weight and do the job I'm being paid for, I'm not prepared to be turned into an on-call round-the-clock drudge. I came here to spend time with you, Auntie Kay.'

Katherine's face shuttered at her niece's words,

and Imogen set her sandwich down and gripped her hands in her lap to counter the painful tightening of her throat. Had she done something to disappoint her aunt, to alienate her somehow? She swallowed hard and did what she could to keep a cheery expression on her face. 'Why did you tell me to get Jasper to help with George? When I dumped the baby on his lap, I thought he was going to pass out. What's the deal with his family?'

Her aunt gave her one of *those* looks. 'Imogen, I don't gossip about my employer.'

'I'm not asking you to. It's just…he seems a bit hung up about it.'

'People's lives can be complicated.'

Was her aunt's life complicated? Was that the problem? 'You think well of him, though, right? I'd even go so far as to say you care what happens to him.'

'I've known him for nearly twenty years. I worked for his family for a long time. Of course I care what happens to him. But he's shut himself away for far too long. It'll do him good to have a bit of contact with the outside world.'

'Are the two of you more than friends?'

Shocked eyes met hers. 'Are you suggesting what I think you're suggesting?'

'I know it's none of my business, but—'

'It most certainly isn't. But, me and Jasper? The idea is ludicrous.'

That made her frown. 'Why? You're both young and attractive. And you're stuck out here together all on your own and—'

'I don't feel *that* young, Imogen, I can assure you. The idea is preposterous. I've known the boy since he was twelve years old.' Katherine's eyes narrowed. 'And I'd advise you not to get any ideas in that direction either. Jasper Coleman is a troubled man. Like the rest of his family.'

'Is there anything I ought to know? Is he…' she hesitated '…dangerous?'

'Of course not. I wouldn't hire any young woman to work here if I thought that, and certainly not my own niece.'

Of course she wouldn't.

'It's just that young women have always fallen all over themselves to impress him. I'd rather not see you join their ranks.'

'Oh, you don't need to worry about me, Auntie Kay. I have plans and I'm not letting any man derail them.' Plans she and her best friend and now business partner, Lauren, had staked their entire life savings on. Elliot could take his *stupid* comments and choke on them, because Imogen *was* going to succeed.

She glanced at her aunt again, swallowed. 'I've been playing around with some new designs and I'd love to show them to you after dinner—get your opinion, throw around some new ideas.' Katherine was the reason she'd learned to sew as a fresh-faced nine-year-old. She'd always encouraged Imogen's creativity.

'I'm sorry, but I have to keep going over the household accounts. I promised Jasper's accountant I'd have them to him by the end of the week.'

It was the same excuse she'd given last night. Imogen did her best to stay chipper, to give her aunt the benefit of the doubt. Maybe she *wasn't* purposely avoiding her. 'Can I help?'

'I expect you're going to have your hands full tonight.' She handed George over. 'Time for me to get back to work.' With that, she strode in the direction of her office.

Imogen watched her go and pursed her lips. As soon as her mother had found out that Katherine was looking for a temporary maid, she'd badgered Imogen to take the position and make sure all was well. And for the first time Imogen was glad she'd promised to do what she could.

Because her mother was right—something was wrong.

She stared down at the now content baby. 'I'm going to get to the bottom of this, George.' Her aunt was acting out of character, and she was going to find out why.

'Are you sure this is the first time you've changed a nappy?' Imogen demanded, moving in to run a finger around the waist and legs of the nappy Jasper had just put on the baby.

She smelled of oranges and vanilla. He frowned; dumbfounded that he'd even noticed what she smelled like. 'The very first time,' he promised, edging away a fraction.

Chagrin flashed across her face and it almost made him smile. So far today he'd learned how to prepare a bottle of formula, though he'd managed to get out of feeding and burping the baby. She'd accepted his 'I'd prefer to watch the first time' excuses, though he doubted he'd get away with that at lunchtime, especially as she'd given him a free pass for the entirety of yesterday. He'd told her he'd needed to put some work measures in place before he could concentrate more fully on helping her with the baby.

It had been a lie, mostly. He owned the company. He employed other people to manage its day-to-day operations. He didn't need to check in daily. A simple email had taken care of business.

But he'd needed the solitude—had needed to get his head around the events of the previous day. Hc'd need a whole lot more than a day and a half of solitude to make that happen, though.

He forced himself back to the present moment to find Imogen still staring at his nappy attempt. 'What? There's nothing wrong with it.'

'I know. That's the problem.' She wrinkled her nose. 'You're one of these perfect people who get everything spot-on first time, aren't you?'

Nope, that didn't describe him at all. 'I'm good with my hands.' Hc'd allow that much. He'd spent far too much time as a kid making paper planes and kites. He'd eventually graduated to assembling model airplanes and ships, and then disassembling computer motherboards and putting them back together—activities that had kept him out of sight and out of the line of his father's fury.

The baby chose that moment to wave his hands in the air with a series of excited gurgles, and Imogen swooped down to kiss those little fists and tickle his tummy, making him chortle. He was a sturdy and happy little chap. *Not* what he'd have expected from Emily's child.

Imogen sent Jasper a sidelong glance, the green in her eyes sparkling with devilment. 'So, you're *good with your hands*, huh?'

He didn't have a collar on his T-shirt, so it had to be an imaginary collar that tightened about his throat. 'I, uh…'

She straightened, laughing outright. 'When I first met you, I dubbed you Mr Cool and Mysterious, but I think I need to revise that to Mr Clueless and Out of His Depth.'

He stiffened, trying to resist the pull of her teasing. 'I *am* still your employer, remember?' But his words didn't carry even a quarter of the weight he'd meant them to.

'Yes, sir!'

She saluted and all he could do was shake his head. Where did all of her irrepressible sense of fun come from?

She stepped away from the change table. If nothing else, the baby had certainly arrived well equipped.

His jaw suddenly clenched. A change table. In his house. On an almost deserted island. It'd look as if he'd planned for the arrival of this child.

Try explaining that to a jury.

'Right, seeing as though you're so good with

your hands, you can carry George through to the living room.'

He crashed back and pushed his dark suspicions to the back of his mind.

He hadn't had to pick the baby up yet. Other than the time she'd plonked him on his lap, he hadn't touched him until the nappy change. Jasper had spent the last two nights at the other end of the house from Imogen and the baby, but Imogen had been adamant this morning that they set up a proper nursery in one of the upstairs guest bedrooms. At *his* end of the house. He'd wanted to protest, but on what grounds?

He couldn't keep taking advantage of Imogen's good nature. And the light in her eyes had told him not to bother trying. She might have an irrepressible sense of fun, but if she was anything like Katherine, she'd have a will of steel too. And instinct told him she was definitely cast in the same mould as her aunt.

So, he'd helped to shift all the associated baby paraphernalia, had unpacked tiny romper suits and little short sets into a chest of drawers. There'd been something about those tiny clothes that'd had his chest clenching. He'd done his best to ignore it. He couldn't afford emotion and sentiment. Not in this situation.

Swallowing back an automatic objection, he took a step closer to the baby.

'What are you afraid of?' she asked softly at his elbow.

Too many things, and all of them too personal to share. But he had to say something. 'I don't want to drop him. I don't want to hurt him.' Both of those things were true.

She didn't laugh, and something inside him unhitched. He suspected he deserved mockery, but he was grateful to be spared it all the same.

'George isn't a newborn, so you don't have to support his head when you lift him. His neck muscles have developed enough to support that weight on their own.'

'Okay.'

'Once you pick him up, you can either balance him on your hip, like you've no doubt seen me doing.'

She seized a teddy bear to demonstrate. He did his best not to focus on the shapely curve of her hip.

'Or you can hold him against your shoulder.' The teddy went to her shoulder where she patted his back. 'Or you can hold him in front of you with his back against your chest.'

The teddy bear was pressed to her chest. But

it was smaller than a life-sized baby and holding the toy there highlighted her, uh…curves. Rather deliciously.

Don't ogle her chest.

'Of course, you shouldn't hold him too tight.'

She demonstrated by pulling the soft toy hard against her and it was all he could do not to groan. He would *not* notice her physical attributes. It'd be wrong on so many levels. He was her employer, for heaven's sake. He might've been stuck on this island for the last two years, but he read the news, kept up with what was happening in the world—the *#metoo* movement had *not* passed him by. And he was not going to join the ranks of men who used their positions of power to prey on young women sexually. The thought sickened him.

He forced his mind back to the task at hand. 'Isn't he going to squirm and throw himself about and…?' He trailed off with a shrug.

'Have you ever held a puppy or kitten?'

'No.' He and Emily hadn't been allowed pets when they were growing up.

He turned to find her mouth had fallen open. A beat started up somewhere in his chest. Her eyes softened and she lifted her hand as if to touch him, and then seemed to recall herself.

Stiffening, she eased back. 'Not everyone is an animal person.'

'I'd have loved a dog as a kid.'

Where on earth had that come from?

But it earned him a smile and he couldn't regret it.

'All I was going to say is that puppies and kittens wriggle a lot when they're excited. George here is a whole lot easier to hold than an over-excited puppy.'

'Okay.'

'So...' She gestured for him to pick up the baby.

He and the baby stared at each other. Carefully, he eased forward and slid his hands beneath the baby's armpits and lifted him. The weight of the baby was somehow reassuring. He dangled him at arm's length, getting used to the weight, noting how large his hands looked around the baby's middle. Little legs kicked as if they had an excess of energy, but they didn't make him feel as if he'd drop the child.

Swallowing, he moved him to rest against his chest and shoulder. The kid grabbed a fistful of Jasper's shirt and bounced, but Jasper kept a hand at the baby's back to steady them both, and then slowly let out a breath. 'Okay, that wasn't so bad.'

He turned to Imogen, expecting to find her smiling, but she wasn't. She was staring at him, hands on hips. 'What?' he asked, suddenly defensive.

'Do you know you haven't spoken to him yet?'

He scowled. Yeah, he knew. It was another one of those threshold moments, and he'd had enough of them for one day. 'Did you have a lot of pets growing up?'

Her face relaxed into a smile. 'I can't imagine not having a dog.'

'You have a dog...*now*?'

She started to laugh. 'Relax, Jasper, I've neither abandoned my dog nor brought her with me and hidden her in your garden shed. She's the family pet, and lives with my parents and has done so for the last ten years. Lulabelle the Labrador cross is adorable and spends most of her days dozing in the sun. I couldn't imagine not having a dog,' she repeated.

He'd ached for a dog as a kid, but he hadn't thought about that in years. He rolled his shoulders, keeping a firm grip on the baby. 'Why not?' What was so good about having a dog?

'They're great company.'

Yeah, well, he didn't need any of that. He liked his own company.

'They're a lot of fun.'

He didn't need fun either.

'And they don't judge you. They just love you unconditionally.'

He couldn't think of anything to say to that.

She started to laugh again. 'And in addition to all of that they'll keep you on your toes as they chew your shoes, dig up the garden, traipse mud into the house and pee on the carpet. A lot like kids, I guess.'

'Oh, now I'm really going to rush out and get a dog,' he said wryly, trying not to notice the way the ends of her hair danced whenever she laughed.

She sobered and nodded at the baby. 'You're going to need to talk to him.'

Damn. He'd thought he'd distracted her from that. 'Why?' Why did he have to talk to the kid? It'd be in everyone's best interests if he could maintain his distance. He'd make sure the baby's physical needs were met—why couldn't that be enough?

'Because he needs to know he can trust you. Besides, it's friendly and polite.'

He wanted to stop his ears and close his eyes.

'He needs to feel comfortable around you, not frightened or intimidated.'

He pulled in a breath. Okay, her words made sense. He could make small talk with the kid, right? It wouldn't kill him. It wouldn't bring the walls he had firmly in place crashing down. He glanced down to find the baby staring at him. 'Hello, baby.'

George shoved a fist in his mouth and eyeballed him.

'George,' she sighed. 'His name is George.'

A scowl shuffled through him. Who'd chosen the name—Emily or Aaron? 'George is too big a name for a baby—too adult.'

'Which is why I sometimes call him Georgie… or Gorgy Georgie.'

The baby pulled his fist from his mouth to smile at her, but Jasper shook his head. 'I am *not* calling him that.' He must've spoken too loudly, because the baby gave a start. 'Sorry if that offends you,' he muttered, patting the nappy-clad bottom. 'What about kid?' he said, hoping to avert some very loud crying. 'Are you all right with me calling you kid?'

To his utter amazement, the little guy threw his head back and laughed. As if Jasper had just told him the funniest joke he'd ever heard. He tried to stop his chest from puffing up, tried to not feel so pleased when a little hand slapped his chest, right above his heart. 'He's a happy little guy, isn't he? Doesn't seem to cry much.'

Her lips curved into the most bewitching smile that he did his best to ignore. 'You sound surprised.'

'I am.'

'Not all babies fuss and cry a lot.'

But he'd never thought for a single moment that Emily's baby would be one of the contented ones. He pushed the thought aside. 'What now? What are we doing next?'

'We're going to the beach.'

He stiffened. 'You just want to go for a swim. You're going to abandon me on a beach with a baby I barely know, while you get to live it up.'

He took one look at her face and he wished he could haul the words back. He'd planted that idea well and truly in her head, and he could see now that she meant to run with it.

'How very perspicacious of you,' she said, mock sweetly. 'I've been on call with the baby ever since he arrived. I deserve a swim. And I'm not exactly abandoning you. I'll be within shouting distance.'

He tried not to scowl.

'And while I'm swimming you might want to give some thought to how you'd like our schedule to work.'

'What do you mean?'

'I'm not leaving Aunt Katherine with all the housework. I'll need a few hours each day to dedicate to my housekeeping duties. I suspect you'll want a few hours each day to work too.'

Um. 'I...' He didn't know what to say, what to suggest.

'For the moment, I'm just saying think about it.'

She turned and left the room. 'Where are you going?' he hollered after her.

'To put my swimmers on,' she hollered back.

'What am *I* supposed to do?'

She moved back to stand in the doorway. She glanced at the baby and then around the room. 'You'd better pack him a bag—some toys, his teething ring, a blanket...and a hat.' She glanced at him, her eyes tracking across his head, and he had to fight the urge to run his hand across his buzz cut. 'You might want one of those too. I'll bring the sunscreen and some cold drinks,' she tossed over her shoulder before disappearing.

Jasper huffed out a breath. 'You wouldn't believe it from the way she speaks to me, kid, but I'm *her* boss.'

He set the baby carefully into his cot while he gathered a few things together. He found a tiny cotton sunhat and set it on the baby's head.

The baby frowned and pushed it off. 'So… it's going to be like that, is it?' Jasper's hands went to his hips. 'She's going to insist on it, you know.' Shoving the hat in the pocket of his cargo shorts, he hiked the bag over his shoulder, lifted the baby out of the cot, and went to find a hat for himself.

CHAPTER FOUR

IMOGEN CHANGED INTO her swimming costume and tried to make sense of the expressions that had flashed across Jasper's face whenever he'd glanced at his nephew. Consternation was ever present, which she got. But she didn't understand his… She didn't know what to call it—calculation, maybe? As if he viewed his nephew as a piece of problematic computer code he needed to decrypt. Or a to-do list he needed to tick off.

Beneath that, though, she also sensed the wonder George stirred in him. And the fact it was an ever-present threat to his detachment. It was as if Jasper was afraid to care even the slightest little bit for his baby nephew.

Maybe he was, but why? Because of his sister?

She slathered on sunscreen. It was none of her business. She knew that. But if George's sister was an irresponsible piece of work or in some kind of trouble, then little George was going to need someone to rely on. Someone like Jasper.

She snapped the tube of suncream closed with the heel of her hand. Surely Jasper didn't mean to abandon George at the end of all this—just hand him back to his mother when the time came and be done with him? Not without some follow-through. Not without making sure George was going to be okay. He had to maintain some contact with his nephew, even if it proved difficult. Right?

But even as she thought it, she was far from convinced Jasper saw it the same way. In fact, she was almost certain he saw it in a completely opposite light.

'He's a troubled man.'

Her aunt's words played in her mind, and she found herself nodding.

'He's demanding and difficult.'

That had her shaking her head, though. He valued his privacy, and she doubted he'd suffer fools gladly, but he wasn't unreasonable, and while he could be remote and aloof he wasn't surly or supercilious. Those things gave her hope because she hadn't imagined the surprise in his eyes, or the pleasure, when George had smiled at him.

If it hadn't been for those glimpsed flashes of warmth, the thawing she sensed him trying to fight, then she'd...

She jammed a hat to her head.

Then you'd what? She mocked her reflection, rubbing in a dollop of cream still left on her nose. She wasn't making a dent in Katherine's aloofness at the moment, so what impact did she think she could have on Jasper?

The one thing she *could* do was to ensure little George's stay here was as lovely as possible. And she meant to do that to the best of her ability.

Grabbing a tote, she tossed in a T-shirt and the sunscreen, before stalking into the kitchen to grab some cold drinks and a bottle of cold boiled water for George. Katherine, sitting at the kitchen table, gave a start and pushed the letter she was reading back into its envelope and slid it beneath the newspaper.

Imogen's chest tightened, but she pretended she hadn't seen the furtive movement. 'We're heading down to the beach. Want to join us?'

'Imogen, I'm working!'

She seized a couple of pieces of fruit. 'You're entitled to some R & R. And I bet Jasper wouldn't mind. In fact, I expect he'd welcome your company.'

'I'm sorry, Imogen, but even if I wasn't busy, I'm not a fan of the beach and all of that sand.' She eyed the fruit Imogen still held. 'And if you're going to feed any of that banana to the baby, you better pack some wet wipes.' She pointed. 'In that cupboard to the left of the sink.'

With a sigh, she grabbed them and then gathered up her things. She paused in the doorway. 'Auntie Kay, is everything okay?'

'Of course it is,' Katherine said brusquely. 'Why wouldn't it be, you silly child? Now, you'd better get your skates on. Jasper won't like kicking his heels for too long. Enjoy your swim.'

She had no choice but to submit. But as she walked away, her mind raced. She needed to find a way to break through her aunt's atypical reserve. Doing housework and looking after a baby were all well and fine, but she had to remember the real reason she was here on Tesoura.

They spread the blanket in the shade of a stand of palm trees that swayed gently in the breeze like something from every hopeful daydream she'd ever had about tropical islands. 'Smell that glorious sea air, George. Feel how warm it is. Hear the sound of the waves.'

She closed her eyes and inhaled. *Glorious.*

When she opened her eyes, she found Jasper staring at her as if she'd lost her mind. George was clapping and beaming. George was the easiest to deal with, so she kept her gaze on him and clapped too. While she might've addressed the baby, her words had been aimed at the man. She wondered if Jasper ever did relaxed and casual. He might've changed into shorts and a T-shirt, but for all intents and purposes he might as well have still been wearing a suit jacket for all the relaxation he radiated.

Pointing that out, though, would be impertinent, and it'd achieve absolutely nothing. So, she kept on clapping her hands. 'This was the game George and I played last night. For a very long time.'

'Looks riveting.'

'It's just as well babies are so cute, because so much of their care falls into the categories of the mundane and downright boring.'

'Which is the real reason you didn't want to take on the job of full-time nanny?'

There was no censure in his voice, just curiosity, and she found her gaze swinging up. 'Do you think housework is any less boring?'

One shoulder lifted. 'Given the way you do it—dancing and singing off-key at the top of your voice—perhaps.'

His words made her laugh, but his almost-smile had things inside her wobbling. She dragged her gaze away. 'Like I said, I just don't want to lose all my leisure time.' She needed the time and headspace to keep chipping away at her aunt.

'So what now? I get the great good fortune to play the clapping game while you enjoy your said leisure time?'

The question could've sounded sulky and petulant, but it didn't. He just looked—and sounded—at a genuine loss. She made a mental note not to swim for too long. She had no intention of abandoning him, not when he evidently felt so out of his depth. 'There are lots of other games too. For example, we like playing choo-choo trains.' She seized the bright red plastic train and pushed it across the blanket, making train noises.

George pursed his lips and made *choo-choo* sounds too, and then clapped and grinned.

Jasper shook his head. 'I'm *not* doing that.'

Imogen gurgled a laugh at George. 'Uncle Jasper thinks choo-choo trains are beneath his dignity.'

George bent at the waist, leaning towards her to laugh too, laughing because she was laughing. He was the sweetest little guy.

Her employer glared. 'I'm wondering how you got to twenty-five years of age without someone throttling you, Ms Hartley.'

'I'm guessing it's because of my sparkling personality.' She hummed a few bars of 'How Do You Solve a Problem Like Maria?' from *The Sound of Music*. Without giving him time to respond, she pulled the bag he'd packed towards her. 'Right, you have a couple of books here—' the thick cardboard ones that were almost indestructible '—so you can read one of those to him. But you have to point to the picture and say the word. Making the appropriate sound will earn you bonus points.' She pointed to a chicken and made chicken noises.

He opened his mouth, but she pushed the book into his hands before he could speak. 'It also makes the game last longer and that can be a blessing when your hands are sore from the clapping game.'

He didn't sigh, but it looked as if he wanted to.

'First and foremost, you need to keep him safe.'

His shoulders immediately tensed. 'What dangers am I guarding against?'

'Well, he isn't crawling yet, but he can roll and he can do a funny kind of tummy crawl. So he can get himself to the edge of the blanket...and there's all of that sand...and everything he picks up goes in his mouth.'

He nodded. 'No sand eating.'

'Once babies begin to move, they can do so surprisingly quickly.' She pointed to the water behind her.

He pointed a finger at her and then the water. '*Not* going to happen.'

'I know. You'll keep an eagle eye on him.'

He blinked.

'Insects can be a problem too. We don't want him bitten by an ant or stung by a bee or anything along those lines.'

He immediately traced the blanket's perimeter with eyes that made her think of laser beams. She pulled in another of those wobbly breaths. His worry, his vigilance, his desire to do this thing—a thing he apparently didn't want to do—to the very best of his ability, touched something inside her, made it soft and breathless. 'And… um…finally…the sun. We don't want him getting sunburned.'

His hands slammed to his hips. 'Then why don't we just take him back inside where it's safe?'

'Jasper,' she said gently, 'he's *your* nephew. You're free to take him back into the house whenever you want. But how would you feel cooped up inside all day? Besides, there are things you need to protect him from in there too—the sharp edges of coffee tables, making sure he doesn't put something he shouldn't in his mouth.'

He dragged a hand down his face, making her heart twist. 'I'm sorry. It's just…there's a lot to consider.'

And he'd never expected to be in this situation. That much was apparent. She forced her lips upwards. 'If it's any consolation, vitamin D is most excellent for growing bones, and sunscreen will help take care of the sunburn.' She raised an eyebrow. 'As will a hat.'

'It's in my pocket,' he muttered. 'He doesn't like wearing it.'

She didn't say anything, simply poured some sunscreen into her hand. 'I've never put this stuff on a baby before, so it could prove interesting.'

He looked as if he wanted to run away. 'How can I help?'

'I don't know. You might need to hold him. Let's see how we do first.'

She smeared a line of the lotion down George's nose and across each cheek, and started to rub it in. He gave a squeal of outrage and tried to turn his face away, but she was too quick for him. When she did it again, he frowned at her and then he opened his mouth and…well, he yelled at her to stop. It was the only way she could think to describe it, and she found herself laughing. 'He reminded me of you then.'

'I don't frown like that.'

'I beg to differ.'

'And I would certainly never yell at you.' He then seemed to recall that moment in his study when he'd found her sitting in front of his computer, and winced, scrubbing a hand across his hair.

She took pity on him. 'Not without provocation,' she agreed. 'And in George's eyes, sunscreen apparently provides ample provocation.'

His nose curled. 'I can understand that. The stuff is sticky.'

If she didn't still have a handful of sunscreen she'd have slammed her hands to her hips. 'Are you telling me you're not wearing sunscreen?'

'I…' His mouth opened and closed. 'There wasn't time.'

Without thought, she reached across and deposited a liberal amount of lotion to his face. George let loose with a long, 'Ooh!'

'Exactly, Master George, Uncle Jasper needs to set you a good example.' But as she said the words, her stomach was clenching up tighter and tighter. She should never have touched him. What on earth had she been thinking?

She hadn't been thinking. She'd acted on impulse. And in this instance, impulse was bad. *Really bad.*

Or really divine. Depended on which way you wanted to look at it. Beneath her fingers Jasper's skin felt warm and vital, vivid, and the strength of him seeped into her fingers and all the way through to her bones, making her feel buoyant and alive. Which was crazy. The scent of him—warm cotton and cardamom—had an unfamiliar yearning stretching through her.

She couldn't look at him; afraid she'd betray the need racing through her. She stared doggedly at George instead. 'I'm really sorry. I shouldn't have drowned you in suncream, but your nephew is watching this exchange intently. And I'm thinking that if I dab a final bit on your forehead and rub it in, then maybe he'll be a bit more amenable and let me do the same to him.'

'Right.'

That was said through a clenched jaw, and she did her best not to wince. She tried to not feel *him* as she did it, but her fingers were tingling by the time she'd finished.

Little George blinked when she repeated the procedure on him, and frowned, but he didn't squeal or holler.

'Okay.' She gritted her teeth. 'Let's try arms next.'

Without a word, Jasper held out an arm, but she couldn't help noticing the way his eyes had turned remote and distant. Cold. It was all she could do not to shiver.

To her amazement, though, George also held his arm out in imitation of his uncle. Holding her breath, she squirted lotion on both arms—man's and child's. 'Quick,' she murmured to Jasper. 'Give me your other arm.'

Again, George copied, and she laid a line of cream down both arms—one strong and tanned, the other tiny, plump and pale. 'Right, we're ignoring your arms for the moment, Jasper. You take one of George's arms while I do the other. You can rub yours in once we're done.' Which meant she wouldn't have to touch him again.

Without a word, and with quick efficient movements that made her own efforts seem clumsy, Jasper gently rubbed the cream into George's right arm. Wanting to distract George while she did his legs, she said, 'Help Uncle Jasper rub the cream on his arms.'

She gave a quick demonstration, not actually touching Jasper, just pretending to, and George immediately leaned forward and started patting his uncle's arm. Jasper turned to her, his eyes wide. 'He…he understood exactly what you wanted him to do!'

'He's smart…and utterly adorable. And that—' she pointed to his arm '—will keep him occupied for ages.'

While the lotion on Jasper's other arm was about to drip onto the blanket. With an apologetic grimace, she reached across and rubbed it in. The action brought her face in close to his and she wondered if the consternation—the turmoil—in his eyes was reflected in hers. She edged back, her mouth going dry, and the shutters slammed down over his eyes, leaving her confused and flailing.

'I think it's time you went for your swim, Imogen.'

'I think that's a very good idea.' She nodded. 'Before you throttle me.'

Did she imagine it or did his lips just twitch?

She started to untie her sarong and his gaze immediately swung away to focus on the baby. It made her heart thump too hard. She swallowed and forced herself to focus on the reason she'd brought him and the baby out here. 'What are you going to do if he cries?'

* * *

Jasper did his level best to keep his eyes on the baby. Imogen's touch—on his face and his arm— had been innocent, almost absent-minded. But it had woken something inside him, and he desperately wanted to lull it back to sleep. Ogling her, near naked in a swimsuit, would *not* help him achieve that particular objective. Besides, he didn't ogle. He'd never ogled. And he wasn't starting now.

'And here's a hint. Calling for me is the wrong answer.'

Her voice was filled with laughter and he wanted to lean into it, play along, but experience warned him not to. While he might have to face the fact that he could like Imogen Hartley—quite a lot actually—there was no place in his life for her. He'd trusted a woman once—had foolishly come to rely on her, had thought they were a team. But she'd left, frightened off by his father's threats. He didn't blame her for leaving, not for a moment. But it'd taught him two hard lessons. The first—that he couldn't rely on anyone but himself. The second—that it'd be wrong of him to put any woman in a position where she could be hurt by his father.

'Jasper?'

She could whisper his name in a way that made the surface of his skin come alive.

She knelt back down to the blanket in front of him and the baby. 'If you're that uncomfortable with this, I'll stay. I don't have to go for a swim.'

'No, you go for your swim.' He didn't want to deprive her of such an innocent pleasure. She'd been looking forward to it—had definitely earned it—and he'd do whatever he could to facilitate it. He made himself swallow, pulled his face into neat lines. 'I'm just…out of practice at talking to people. Evidently I've been spending too much time in my own head.'

He couldn't believe he'd said that out loud. He wanted to check his words, choke them back, but it was too late. Gritting his teeth, he forced his mind back to her original question. 'If the baby cries, I'll make sure nothing is hurting him, and then I'll check his nappy.' Um… 'I saw a bottle of something in your bag…?'

'It's just cold boiled water.'

Right. 'Well, I'll see if he wants that.'

'And if that doesn't work?'

He tried not to scowl—neither she nor the baby deserved his malcontent. 'I'll distract him by playing choo-choo trains or something equally inane.'

The green flecks in her eyes shone bright and clear. She stared at him steadily now and he didn't know if she was amused by him or concerned.

Don't be an idiot.

If she was concerned about anyone it'd be the baby.

'And if that doesn't work,' he added, doing his best not to frown, 'I'll sing to him.'

Her lips parted. 'What a lovely idea.'

He stared at those parted lips and that monster he'd been trying to lull roared back to life—fierce, hungry and primal. Her eyes widened at whatever she saw in his face, and her tongue eased out to moisten her lips. They stared at each other, lost in some strange in-between world—but in between what he couldn't say—and then the baby squealed, and she jerked back, and he could breathe again.

She leapt to her feet. 'If he cries, pick him up and give him a cuddle. That might be all he needs—a bit of reassurance that he's safe.' And with that, her sarong floated to the ground and she set off towards the water.

He did his best not to notice her bare legs and arms or the curve of her hips. She wore a seriously sedate swimsuit, and a sun shirt. It shouldn't make a man's mouth dry with longing.

It shouldn't.

Keep your head.

He'd been on his own too long, that was all. This was just an…adjustment.

A squeal at his elbow snagged his attention. He glanced down to find the baby pointing a wobbly arm after Imogen and frowning. 'Immy's going for a swim.' He called her Immy to the baby because it was what she called herself. *Come to Immy; Immy's getting your bottle now.*

George looked as if he might cry. 'She'll be back soon. It's not worth getting upset about, kid, believe me. Look—' he held out his arm, shuffling closer '—we haven't rubbed all of this goop in yet.'

The baby gave a toothless grin and started patting Jasper's arm with an enthusiasm that tugged at the older man's heart. He was a clever little kid. Were all babies this smart? He'd bet they weren't.

They spent a leisurely few minutes making sure it was all rubbed in, and then George stared at him expectantly. Right… He cleared his throat. 'Do you want to play the clapping game?' He clapped his hands together a few times. Nothing. 'What about your train?' He seized the train. 'Would you like to play with that?' No way was he making *choo-choo* noises, though.

The train was tossed across the blanket. Uh-huh…

The hat! He pulled it from his pocket and set it on the kid's head. The kid immediately sounded a protest and went to pull it off, but Jasper whipped out his own cap and waved it about.

'Look, I have a hat too.'

And he set it on his own head.

The baby pointed to it and bounced. 'Um! Um! Um!'

He wanted Jasper's hat? He handed it over. The kid pulled his own hat off and gave it to Jasper, and then tried to put Jasper's cap on. He finally managed it, with a bit of help from his uncle, and did his best to look up at Jasper, but the brim covered his eyes. Fat hands lifted the brim, and when he finally made eye contact with Jasper, he laughed hysterically. Jasper couldn't help but laugh too. The kid had a weird sense of humour. And that was the game they played for the next twenty minutes—swapping hats and laughing.

Boring and mundane? Perhaps. But he'd attended board meetings that had dragged worse and achieved less. And at least he was sitting in the sun on a beautiful beach.

The thought gave him pause. Since when did he care where he was or what the weather was like? Though a bit of sun was good for the baby. Imogen had said so. Personally, he didn't care about either the beach or the sunshine. At least that was what he told himself.

He glanced back at the baby. Okay, this whole 'looking after a kid' thing wasn't rocket science. It was something he *could* learn. He could make sure all the kid's physical needs were met, and be friendly with the little guy, *and* keep his distance. He didn't need to engage his emotions towards the baby any more than he did towards his staff back in Sydney. He cared about their well-being, naturally, but it didn't matter to him on a personal level if they decided to leave his employment or anything. Just as it wouldn't matter when Emily demanded the return of her child.

And as far as Jasper was concerned, that was the best-case scenario he could think of.

'Look.' He pointed down the beach. 'Here comes Immy.' She moved with an unconscious grace that had his chest drawing tight, making it hard to get air into his lungs. He swallowed and looked away. 'I hope she enjoyed her swim, kid. She's earned it.' He had to do better where she was concerned. She'd gone above and beyond these last two days.

George glanced up at Jasper, eyes wide, and then his face split into a grin and he clapped his hands. Jasper found himself smiling back and clapping his hands too.

'How was the water?' he asked when she reached them, doing his best to look—and feel—unaffected.

'Freezing!' she said with her usual irrepressible cheerfulness, grabbing her towel and drying her face. 'Makes you tingle all over.'

Tingling was the last thing he needed to think about, but she literally glowed from her swim. Something inside him responded to it. And there was nothing he could do about it. Other than try and ignore it.

'Hey, Georgie, did you have fun?' And then she squeezed a drop of water from her hair and let it fall to the baby's foot.

George squealed. And when she made as if to drip more water on him, he squealed louder, seized a handful of Jasper's shirt and hauled himself upright on wobbly legs. He'd have fallen, would've pitched forward to smack his face against Jasper's knees, if Jasper hadn't caught him. The kid then stood balanced on Jasper's lap, and he bounced and chortled and waved his arms in glee that he'd evaded Imogen and her antics.

Jasper could barely draw breath. The baby had *trusted* him to catch him—to protect him and keep him safe.

George laughed up at his uncle now as if they'd shared a joke. Jasper's mouth dried. That...that was just fanciful, right? Nine-month-old babies couldn't share a joke with you.

The baby's legs gave way, and he plopped down on Jasper's knee, snuggling into him...and then he wrapped an arm across Jasper's tummy and he cuddled him. Every hard thing inside Jasper's heart melted to a puddle, and his arms went around little George of their own volition.

He stared down at his nephew, his heart filling with too much emotion. He said the rudest word he knew. Very softly.

He glanced up to find Imogen watching. She didn't remonstrate with him for his bad language. Instead, she asked, 'What just happened?'

The soft warmth of her voice helped to soothe the ragged edges of the panic pounding through him.

He didn't bother trying to deny it. 'I'm falling for him.'

She wrapped her towel about herself and sat on the edge of the blanket. 'What's wrong with that?'

His chest ached. His throat ached. And his head pounded. 'I have absolutely no jurisdiction over this child, Imogen. When one of his parents demands his return, I have to hand him over. I won't be able to keep George here.'

She sucked her bottom lip into her mouth, her gaze never leaving his. 'But you can visit him, can't you? And he can come for holidays here to Tesoura, right?' She searched his face. 'I'm not getting something. What am I not getting?'

A breath rattled out of him. 'My sister is married to a man who beats her. I tried to help her break free of him, but she didn't want that. Instead, she cut *me* from her life and said she never wanted to see me again.'

Her hand flew to her mouth. When her gaze lowered to the babe in his arms, her eyes filled. He wanted to hug her for her concern, for the way she worried about George. For her kindness.

'No matter how much I might want to, I can't protect George. Not from his own parents.' And yet how on earth could he abandon George to a lifetime of fear and abuse?

Nausea churned through him. History was

going to repeat, and he was powerless to stop it. The thought nearly broke him.

'Despite all of that,' Imogen said slowly, 'your sister still sent the baby to you. That has to mean something, don't you think? What did her letter say?'

'Next to nothing!' It hadn't provided him with an ounce of reassurance. George jumped at his tone and started to fidget, Jasper soothed him the way he'd seen Imogen doing—holding him against his shoulder and rubbing his back. '"Dear Jasper,"' he recited through gritted teeth, '"I know you've probably not forgiven me, but there are some things I need to take care of. In the meantime, I need someone to look after George. Please keep him safe until I can come for him. Emily."'

She hadn't signed off with 'love' or 'best wishes' or 'sincerely' or anything else. And she hadn't given him any further explanation. He wasn't sure why he'd expected more. His lips twisted. Hope sprang eternal, he supposed.

Imogen had stiffened. She stared straight at him as if expecting something more from him—in the same way he'd expected something more from Emily. 'What?'

'It sounds like she's in trouble.'

He hated the way her words made his gut clench. 'What makes you think that?'

Her hands lifted. 'What makes you think there could be any other possible explanation?'

'Experience.'

She blinked and eased back. He was going to have to explain, and he didn't want to. But George needed all the allies he could get, and Jasper had no intention of ostracising a potential ally as kind and generous as Imogen. She made his nephew smile and she made him feel safe. That was worth more than gold.

He did what he could to find his equilibrium. 'My father and brother-in-law are both shaped in the same mould.'

Her bottom lip wobbled. 'They're both...violent?'

'They're both miserable excuses for human beings.'

Her eyes filled again, and it made his chest twist. 'I can't stand either one of them,' she said with quiet vehemence, and for some reason it warmed up parts of him that had started to chill.

'My father wanted all of my mother's attention. He resented Emily and me for taking up so much of her time. Sometimes, when it all got a bit too much for her, she'd farm us out to relatives for a couple of weeks or would send us off to some holiday camp.'

He'd hated it, but at the same time he'd welcomed the reprieve from his father's anger.

Imogen worried at her lip. 'She was probably trying to protect you.'

His head felt too heavy for his shoulders. 'Or saving her own skin.' And he didn't blame her. But when he'd offered her a chance to escape her husband—when he'd offered her refuge and a chance to start a new life—she'd spurned it, had rejected him. Just like Emily.

'That's what you think Emily is doing with George?'

'I know that on the day she sent George here, she and Aaron attended a big charity ball in Sydney—one of the biggest events of the social calendar—filled with all of the powerful and well-to-do. I also know that in the coming week Aaron is going to the States. No doubt Emily will be going with him.'

She pressed a hand to her brow. 'What if you're wrong? What if she's in trouble and trying to break away from her husband? Him going to the States could provide her with the perfect opportunity to do that. Does she have anyone she can turn to? Would your parents take her in?'

'My father would order her to return to Aaron.' The two of them had always been as thick as thieves.

'Friends?'

'Aaron vets all of her friends—in truth he's probably isolated her from them all by now.' In the same way his father had his mother.

'So she has no one to turn to?'

She had him! She had her brother. He broke out in a cold sweat. Despite everything she had to know that, didn't she?

CHAPTER FIVE

'I'VE BEEN THINKING about what you said.'

Jasper came striding down the path towards her and Imogen halted in her pegging out of George's tiny clothes, momentarily transfixed. The back garden was a riot of shrubs, palms and flowerbeds, but none of that could hold a candle to the man moving with such easy grace towards her.

He carried George in his arms, completely at ease as if he'd been born to it. The image of a little baby held against a pair of broad, sigh-worthy shoulders—all of George's small helplessness contrasted with Jasper's power and strength—had the potential to do crazy things to a woman's insides. Protectiveness and nurturance all wrapped up in a single glorious package. Was there anything more attractive—?

She broke off, realising that Jasper was staring at her expectantly. She tried to click her mind into gear. 'You've been thinking about what I said?' she parroted, hoping she didn't look completely at sea.

'About Emily.'

She eased back to survey him more fully. 'About the possibility of her being in trouble?'

He nodded.

She glanced at George, currently fascinated by a bird singing in a nearby shrub, before turning back to Jasper with his serious grey eyes and mouth that was made for smiling but so rarely did. She was becoming too invested here, but how could she not? The way these two had bonded in the last couple of days amazed her. They adored each other. And it made her fear for them both.

She swallowed. 'And…?'

'I have a favour to ask.'

Her heart leapt. Which made no sense. She bent down to retrieve a tiny pair of shorts from the laundry basket. 'Okay.'

He took the shorts from her and handed her George. 'I need your help.'

'Okay.' She focussed on the variety of romper suits, bibs and singlets that waved in the breeze like colourful bunting and tried to get her racing pulse under control.

He pegged out the shorts and then reached into

the basket for a bib and pegged it out too. She wanted to tell him that she was paid to do the laundry, but didn't because…well, he was the boss and she guessed he was also paying her to hold the baby.

'Does that mean you'll help?'

'Of course I will.' A woman could be in trouble, and there was a baby involved. How could she refuse?

And just maybe the warmth from a pair of grey eyes as they rested on her didn't hurt either.

That's shallow, Imogen. Seriously shallow.

But Jasper's eyes *weren't* shallow. They hinted at depths she found intriguing…fascinating.

He reached out and clasped her forearm in silent thanks. The heat of his touch penetrated through skin, muscle and sinew, making her want more. She sucked in a breath as the ground beneath her feet shifted. It took her so off guard she didn't have time to hide her reaction. His gaze narrowed and his nostrils flared. She recognised the same need and hunger coursing through his eyes.

Everything inside her clenched. She forgot to breathe.

He stepped back, distancing himself behind a mask of stern calmness, and she gulped in a breath, reminding herself that he was her employer and she was his employee. And even if that weren't the case she wasn't getting involved with someone who'd marooned himself on a desert island.

She had plans. Lauren was relying on her. She was relying on Lauren. As soon as she left here she was throwing herself wholeheartedly into those plans. If she didn't she and Lauren would lose everything they'd worked and saved so hard for—it wasn't just her money they were risking, but Lauren's too. They'd made a solemn promise to give this new business of theirs every chance they could—to give it their very best efforts. She squared her shoulders. She wasn't letting Lauren down, and she *would* prove the naysayers wrong.

Tesoura was idyllic for some holiday R & R, but there was no way she'd ever live in a place like this.

Not that he'd ever ask her to.

Which was exactly as it should be.

She retreated to a nearby stone bench and busied herself bouncing the baby. Tried to quieten the clamour flooding her veins.

'I didn't realise how much laundry a baby could generate.'

Jasper surveyed George's clothes flapping in

the breeze, obviously not finding it difficult to move on from thoughts of touching her. Well, she could move on too—with the same super-duper ease. She pasted on a bright smile, which admittedly was a little difficult when she was gritting her teeth, and tickled George's stomach. 'Messy little tyke, aren't you?'

Jasper continued pegging out the clothes. She kept her gaze trained on a nearby hibiscus flower in bright red.

'Is there a trick to it?'

Jasper, with the now empty basket clasped to his side, starcd at her. She moistened dry lips. 'A trick to what?'

'Washing George's clothes.'

She tried to stop her eyes from staring. 'You want to do the laundry?'

'*Want* is too strong a word, but you said you'd teach me everything I needed to know. I want to know how to do it *all*. And it doesn't seem fair that you get landed with all the boring, mundane bits.'

That was the problem. Right there. In that one gloriously generous sentence. He said something like that, and it turned her to mush. He acted all lord of the manor one moment, and then...and then the opposite of that. It could knock a girl sideways if she was taken unawares. She did what she could to stiffen a backbone that wanted to melt. 'Jasper, stuff like doing the laundry is what you're paying me for.'

'But if something were to happen to you or Katherine—say you both got a tummy bug—or were simply busy with other things, I'd need to know how to do something as basic as wash George's things.'

She knew he came from a privileged background, but surely he knew the fundamentals. 'You, um…have done a load of washing before, right?'

He looked momentarily horrified, and then he laughed. 'It's true that my family had household staff when I was growing up, but seriously, Imogen. Your aunt was my family's housekeeper for nearly twenty years. What do you think?'

She bit back a grin. 'I expect she made sure you and your sister learned a few life skills.'

'Precisely. I know how to operate my washing machine. I do my own laundry when your aunt takes her annual leave.'

Why hadn't he granted her leave at Christmastime? The more she learned about him, the more of a puzzle that became. She couldn't imagine him denying her aunt any request for leave.

Which maybe meant Katherine had lied to them. It maybe meant her aunt hadn't wanted to spend Christmas with her family.

She swallowed.

'Imogen?'

She shook herself. 'The only difference is in the laundry powder. We use a milder detergent for George's things. A baby's skin is more sensitive than an adult's.' She led him into the laundry room where she pointed the relevant washing powder out to him.

He nodded. 'Okay, got it.'

The laundry was generous by laundry room standards, but far too small to be confined in with Jasper and her own see-sawing hormones. Especially when he leaned in close to take George from her arms. The scent of warm spice invaded her senses. She took a hasty step back and spun on her heel to lead the way into the kitchen. 'So how can I help? What's this favour you want to ask?'

'I want to set up a fake social media account. I've spent the last two days trying to contact Emily, but with no luck. It could be that she's simply wanting to avoid me.'

The worry in his eyes belied that, though, and

it tugged at her heart. 'You think you'll be able to reach her via social media?'

'It's worth a shot. I suspect Aaron monitors all her phone calls and social media accounts. He'd never allow her to friend me or anyone associated with me.'

She still wasn't a hundred per cent sure what this had to do with her.

'But he probably wouldn't look twice if she received a friend request from Jupiter Collins, who attends the same gym.'

The penny dropped. 'You want me to pose on social media as Jupiter Collins.'

'Complete with a profile pic, history and a social calendar filled with all the things young women your age like to do.'

'I already have social media accounts, though. My picture is already out there in cyberspace. Won't that...' she lifted her hands '...cause problems, blow our cover?'

'I have computer programs that will help with that. When I'm finished with your picture, you won't recognise yourself.'

'Okay, let's do this.'

They left the baby with Katherine. Once in his office, the first thing Jasper did was position Imogen against a wall without windows, so there was no possibility of the view giving away their location, and took a photo.

She watched in amazement as he hunkered down at the computer with her image before him on the screen and changed her dark brown hair—all wild curls—to a sleek blonde shoulder-length bob. Her hazel eyes became blue and he lightened her skin tone. She tried not to grimace as he then did odd things, like lengthen her face, widen her smile and enlarge her eyes.

She pressed her fingers to her face, to reassure herself that everything there was unchanged. 'Me, but not me. It's amazing.'

Jasper studied the image on his screen. 'I like the real you better.'

'Yeah, right,' she snorted. 'She's thinner, has beach-blonde hair and big baby blues. And is a gym junkie!'

Jasper laughed, and for a moment it felt as if she were catching a big wonderful wave that rolled you gently all the way to shore. 'While you're sassy, funny and cute. And a surf junkie.'

He thought she was cute? Really?

She tossed her hair. '*Sassy* is just another word for "lack of subservience", right?'

He chuckled again, his fingers typing away furiously. 'I'm not all that interested in subservience, Imogen. Your good heart is of far more value to me.'

Don't melt. Don't melt.

He suddenly froze. 'This—' he gestured to the screen '—isn't some weird male fantasy of mine. I wouldn't want you thinking that this is a… I mean…'

She took pity on him. 'That's good to know, Jasper.'

He eyed her uncertainly and then turned back to his computer. 'I made up a short bio for our Ms Collins last night.'

Jupiter Collins's biography appeared on the screen, and Imogen leaned in closer to read it.

'I have her living in a neighbouring Sydney suburb to Emily, and she goes to the same gym. I made her five years younger so they can't be old school friends.'

She read the bio, and something tugged at her. 'Give her a baby too.'

'Why?'

'So, we can tell her how George is doing.'

He swung to her. 'That's a really nice idea. Boy or girl?'

'Girl.'

'Name?'

'Georgia,' she said immediately. 'Georgia…

Jas…' She tried to think of a feminine version of Jasper. 'Jasmine! Georgia Jasmine.'

He huffed out a laugh but sobered almost immediately. 'A baby will provide another point of contact. They both go to the gym *and* have babies of a similar age. Jupiter's friend request shouldn't raise Aaron's suspicions.'

His fingers flew across the keyboard. They looked sure and capable and she'd never realised before how sexy a man's hands could be. The thought of those hands on her body—

Heat exploded through her and she had to look away.

Inappropriate. Seriously inappropriate.

'How…um…?' She cleared her throat. 'If you and your sister are estranged, how do you know what gym she goes to?'

'I rang her best friend yesterday.'

He'd been busy.

'Aaron hates Prue. Has forbidden Emily from having anything to do with her.'

Imogen's nose curled. 'I *really* don't like this man.'

'I hate him.'

He slumped as if all the energy had drained from him at that admission. Imogen found herself reaching out to clasp his hand.

'You're doing what you can. You're keeping George safe and you're giving Emily a way to contact you if she needs to. One step at a time.'

His hand tightened about hers. 'I shouldn't have leapt to conclusions so quickly—shouldn't have been so caught up in my own bitterness that I discounted the possibility that she might be in trouble.'

He glanced at their joined hands and then released her so fast it made her blink. She pulled her hand into her lap, her heart starting to pound. 'What matters is that you're doing something now.'

He went back to his typing, his mouth set in a straight line. 'Emily and Prue *accidentally* bump into each other every once in a while. Prue makes sure of it. She agrees with you, by the way. She said the only reason Emily would send George away was if something was wrong.'

And he'd immediately leapt into action to help a sister who hadn't spoken to him in two years.

'I'm giving Jupiter three months' worth of history.'

'How on earth can you do that if you're only creating the profile today?'

He glanced at her from beneath his brow. 'It's probably better not to ask.'

Right.

'Any suggestions for things Jupiter might've posted?' he asked.

'Absolutely.'

The corners of his mouth twitched. 'You didn't hesitate.'

'I'm a very social person. I have a phone full of photos that I've shared on social media.'

'Social, huh?'

'I take pictures of movies I've seen, books I'm reading—usually for my book club—pictures of my toes after I've had a pedicure. Cocktails make great pictures to share. And the beach. I share oodles of pictures of the beach. And my softball team's scores.'

'You play softball?'

'Yep. It's off-season at the moment, but I'm a halfway decent hitter and—' she waggled her eyebrows '—I'm third base.'

'You don't say?' Those delicious lips curved upwards. 'You lead a full life.' The smile faded and his brow knitted together. 'You must hate it here.'

What on earth…? 'Of course I don't hate it. Tesoura is paradise, and Aunt Katherine is here. It's the perfect spot for a mini-break.'

'But you'd never settle in a place like this for good?'

'No way. I'd holiday here again in a heartbeat. But I couldn't live the kind of life you do, Jasper. I love my softball team and my book club. I'd miss my family and friends too much. I love my life. Why would I give all that up? Even for an island paradise?'

I love my life. Imogen's words rang through Jasper's mind. Had he ever loved his life?

The answer came swift and sure. *No.*

He'd been fiercely glad when, at the age of eighteen, he'd broken away from his father's control. In retaliation, Keith Coleman had refused to pay for his son's university studies, had refused to introduce him to the so-called 'right people' and had refused to put his name forward at his exclusive gentlemen's club. Jasper didn't regret any of it.

He'd used the modest legacy his grandmother had left him to help fund his studies. He'd worked part-time and had flat-shared with three other guys. He'd got by just fine.

He'd loved being free of his father. But he hadn't loved his life. His victory had been bittersweet. Neither his mother nor Emily had ever managed to escape, despite all of his begging, despite the detailed plans he'd given them to prove they could make it work. He'd had to continue watching from the sidelines as his father had directed their lives with a filthy temper and an iron fist.

At the age of twenty-five he'd invented a universal print drive that had made him millions. He'd renewed his petitions to his mother and Emily to come and live with him, or to let him buy them houses of their own away from Keith and Aaron. He'd promised them money and whatever else they needed, had sworn to protect them. But again, they'd both refused.

And then everything had blown up in his face and…

And he'd come here.

Luckily he'd had the means to do that!

But while he'd been free, he hadn't been happy.

His money meant he'd been able to put together a crack team of computer programmers. His company made some of the market's bestselling computer games. That gave him satisfaction. There'd been a couple of women he'd imagined himself in love with over the years. Those affairs had been exciting. But he'd never experienced the kind of bone-deep contentment with his life that Imogen evidently did with hers.

And while a part of him envied it, he also suspected a life like that could never be his. A person needed a better childhood than he'd had to achieve that kind of happiness—the sense of security that such happiness could last and was worth investing in.

It was a timely reminder of the gulf that lay between him and his intriguing part-time nanny. He was in danger of finding her too interesting, too...*desirable*. And he needed to annihilate all thoughts in that direction. Mentally girding his loins, he glanced across to find her scrolling through pictures on her phone.

'I can't use photos you've already uploaded to social media,' he felt bound to point out.

'But there are oodles and oodles that I haven't used. I took some of the gardens in the local park.'

They'd be suitably generic. Jupiter could be interested in gardening. Excellent.

'Here's a lovely glass of Sémillon.'

She liked Sémillon?

'Wait, what was that?' He touched her wrist as a couple of photos whizzed past.

She went back and a picture of a formal dress appeared. 'This?' She turned the screen more fully towards him. 'We're not sharing that. It's one of my new designs. I've been snapping the odd shot to share when I open my school in May.'

He sat back. He didn't know why he was so shocked. 'You're a designer?' On some level he'd always known she wasn't actually a housemaid, but... 'You're opening a design school?'

'I'm a dressmaker,' she corrected. 'And it's more a sewing school than a design school. We'll teach sewing, dressmaking, pattern making and so forth. We'll also offer a bespoke dressmaking service.' She shrugged. 'We're hoping it'll keep us busy.'

'Us?'

'A girlfriend and I are going into partnership.'

'Why are you waiting till May? Why not now?'

'The premises we've leased don't become available until then. And Lauren is on contract in the UK until March, so...'

He didn't know what to say. 'I had no idea.'

'There's absolutely no reason why you should.' That cheeky smile peeped out, making things inside his chest fizz like champagne. 'So maybe now you can see why I have such a problem with subservience. I actually want to be the big ka-huna.'

She winked as she said it, though, and he knew she was simply teasing him. But… 'Launching a brand-new business. It's—' He snapped his mouth shut.

None of his business.

Those green sparkles in her eyes dimmed as if she knew exactly what he was going to say. 'Why aren't I back home frantically preparing for the launch of my school?' She started flicking through her photos again, but her knuckles had turned white. 'Lauren and I have been working towards this launch for two years. We've got everything in place, ready to go. I'll be back home in March, maybe sooner, to do all the pre-launch stuff.' She glanced up as if she was going to say more, but then shrugged. 'This will be my last chance for some R & R for some time to come, I expect. I mean to enjoy it while I can.'

But she wasn't getting R & R, was she? She was working as a maid and nanny. He glanced at his watch.

The woman opposite him gurgled back a laugh. 'Is there somewhere you need to be?'

He liked her laugh, and he liked it when he could make her laugh. He pulled in a breath—

mentally pulling back. He had no intention of getting too used to that laugh. It was a temporary treat, like ice cream or cake.

When was the last time you had ice cream?

He rolled his shoulders. That didn't matter. It just proved how easy it was to give up unnecessary treats—like ice cream, cake and a woman's smile—and not miss them. And he had no intention of missing Imogen when she was gone either.

In one sudden swift movement, she pushed away from his desk. 'Oh, you probably are busy! Probably have video conference calls planned and all manner of things. I—'

'Not today,' he assured her. 'I just wanted to make sure we weren't running late for your daily swim.'

She eased back down into the chair. 'You don't have to work that into your schedule, Jasper. It's my job to work around yours.'

She was already going above and beyond. And he didn't like the thought of her swimming on her own. He didn't say those things out loud. He simply said, 'George enjoys his time on the beach.'

She looked as if she wanted to say something but turned back to her phone instead.

'What were you going to say?'

The green lights in her eyes caught the sun pouring in at the windows, and it made him suddenly glad that he'd chosen to live on a tropical island rather than some frozen rock in the North Sea.

'Just that we can take it in turns if you like? Swimming, I mean. You have this amazing beach at your disposal. Why not take advantage of it? It's way more fun than laps.'

For the past two years he'd exercised—hard. But he'd chosen the gruelling and effective over the fun. He hadn't felt like having fun. But today her suggestion appealed. 'You wouldn't mind?'

Luscious lips broke into a broad smile. 'Would I mind sitting on the beach, here in paradise, playing with George while you have a dip in the ocean?' She shook her head. 'You're a seriously hard taskmaster, Mr Coleman, but I'm up for that particular challenge.'

He tried not to grin. And failed.

She rested her chin on her hands and pursed her lips. 'I don't have the subservient thing down, but you don't really have the boss thing down either, do you?'

'My philosophy is to hire the best people, tell

them what I want, and then leave them to get on with it. I find that works ninety-nine per cent of the time.'

'Nice philosophy.'

She gazed at him with frank admiration and it made perspiration gather at his nape. 'It doesn't mean I can't pull rank when I need to.'

'I already know this about you.'

Damn. Was she never going to let him forget that unfortunate morning when he'd growled at her? He opened his mouth to apologise—*again*—when he recognised the teasing laughter in her eyes and something inside him eased. 'Very funny, Ms Hartley. Now if you'd be kind enough to send me some of those photos…?'

She turned her attention back to her phone. 'I'm sending them with captions.'

'Because you don't think I can manage a twenty-five-year-old woman's voice?'

'Because it'll be quicker, and I want to get down to the beach.'

'That definitely wasn't subservient.'

He was rewarded with a tinkle of delighted laughter as he watched his email program and waited for the first of her photos to come through. They hit his inbox in quick succession. Her captions were short and sparky and the voice was better—younger—than he could've ever managed.

'So?'

She stared at him with an angled chin, evidently waiting for feedback. He was a firm believer in giving praise where it was due. 'These are perfect.'

'I should've been a writer.'

For a fraction of a second, he stilled. Did she know Katherine's secret? Had her aunt finally confided in her? Whether she had or hadn't, it wasn't his place to give the game away. 'It's not too late,' he said instead. 'Though you might be pressed for time with the opening of your new school.'

'Yeah, nah.'

His lips twitched. 'Was that a yes or a no?'

'It's a maybe.'

She'd gone back to her phone and an influx of new pictures arrived, along with suggestions for status updates. All spot on and useful. He suddenly frowned. 'Would it be asking too much for me to have a look at your profile?'

'Friend me.'

Not a good idea.

Her fingers stilled. She glanced up. 'You don't have a profile on social media, do you?'

'No.'

'Of course he doesn't,' she murmured, before gesturing to his keyboard. He opened another browser window and handed the keyboard over, careful to glance away when she typed in her password. Her feed promptly appeared on his screen and as he scrolled down it, he found it as fun and vibrant as the woman herself.

He let out a breath. 'You and Jupiter don't sound anything alike.' It was the reason he'd wanted to check her account.

Liar. You wanted a voyeuristic glimpse into that life she loves.

'You made it pretty clear you didn't want anyone being able to trace Jupiter to me—or to link us together in any way.'

'I wish some of the people I work with were as quick to read between the lines as you.'

'Ooh, do I sense a promotion to Marketing Manager?'

'Not a chance.' He channelled his best Captain Von Trapp impression to counter the overwhelming desire to reach across and slam his lips to hers. 'Way too much trouble for the abbey.'

She didn't laugh as he'd expected. Her gaze

was focussed on the computer. She pointed. 'That's my family. At Christmas. The holiday is a big deal for us.'

She had a big extended family. And every person in the photograph wore a big grin and a silly paper hat—the kind that came from Christmas crackers. There were pictures of huge platters of king prawns sitting either side of a baked ham that held pride of place on a table groaning with baked vegetables and salads. There were pictures of a game of backyard cricket and a water fight. It was about as far from the Christmases of his childhood as one could get.

He thought of George and his heart burned. What would his nephew's future Christmases be like?

'Of course, Aunt Katherine wasn't there, which put a bit of a dampener on things.'

Katherine hadn't been there? Why not? She'd told him—

He gulped the question back and glanced up to find Imogen… Well, she wasn't actually glaring at him, but it was only one level away. There was definitely puzzlement in those eyes, and a lurking resentment.

Katherine hadn't been at the Hartley family Christmas.

And Imogen blamed him for it. *He's difficult and demanding.*

'What do you do for Christmas, Jasper?'

'Nothing.'

She straightened. 'What, really? Nothing? No roast turkey or ham or…or a plum pudding or presents?'

'Nothing,' he repeated, a bad taste coating his tongue.

'You don't have your bachelor buddies come to stay or…or…?'

'Nothing.'

The single word sounded stark.

It *was* stark.

He glanced back at the photographs on the screen. All that laughter and fun… He could never re-create that in a million years—he wouldn't know where to start—but in the future he could at least make an effort. He had to. For George's sake.

'What happened to you, Jasper?'

He glanced across at her whispered words. Her eyes had welled with such sadness he reached out to touch her cheek, aching to offer her some form of comfort. He wanted to tell her not to cry for him, but the words wouldn't come.

He pulled his hand back and lifted his chin.

'Nothing of any note.' It'd be better for her to not get involved in his life. Much better. 'C'mon, it must be time for that swim.'

CHAPTER SIX

IMOGEN SLATHERED SUNSCREEN across her cheeks,
surreptitiously watching her aunt as the older
woman jiggled George on her knee. Despite
Katherine's no-nonsense briskness and seemingly cheerful demeanour, it couldn't hide the
tired lines stretching from her eyes or the occasional slump of her shoulders when she thought
no one was watching.

Ever since Imogen had arrived on the island,
she'd told herself to go slow, that there was time
for her to win her aunt's confidence, but she was
coming to the conclusion that she'd chosen the
wrong approach.

Except…

Her chest squeezed tight. Except the expression on Jasper's face when she'd blurted out her
question not ten minutes ago—*what happened
to you?*—had shown her the folly of the direct
approach.

The darkness that had stretched through his

eyes… It had made her throat burn and her eyes sting. She'd have done anything in that moment to make him feel better.

That's not what you're here for.

With a sigh, she glanced at her aunt, who was playing some game with George that involved his fingers and toes. 'Auntie Kay, what made you come to Tesoura?'

Katherine raised an eyebrow. 'I didn't want to work for Keith Coleman any more. I liked his wife, and I'd liked both Emily and Jasper, but they'd left home by then…' She ran a gentle hand over George's hair. 'And after the blow-up, I thought Jasper could use a friendly face.'

She plonked herself in a seat. 'What blow-up?'

'Honestly, Imogen, it was in all the papers at the time.' Her aunt turned to face her more fully. 'Your lack of interest in current affairs is appalling.'

She wrinkled her nose. 'I keep abreast of world affairs. And two years ago, I was in Paris.' She'd been doing an internship at one of the big fashion houses there. Australian news didn't rate much more than a line or two in the European papers. She racked her brain for what her mother must've told her at the time, but she'd been so full of the excitement of living and working in Paris—all that she'd been learning and experiencing—that if her mother had told her anything, it certainly hadn't stuck.

'There was a falling out between Jasper and the rest of his family. His brother-in-law accused him of assault and Jasper was charged—it was all set to go to court—but the charges were dropped.'

Her heart hammered against her ribs. 'And?'

'And that's all anyone knows. Other than the fact that none of them have spoken to Jasper since. Or he to them.'

Had Jasper given his brother-in-law a taste of his own medicine? She hoped so. She *really* hoped so.

'But as Keith is one of Australia's leading politicians, the tabloids had a field day with the story—it seemed that every day there were front pages splashed with claims and counter claims. It was ugly, and an unpleasant time for the family.'

No wonder Jasper had leapt to the wrong conclusion the day he'd found her sitting at his computer chortling, *Eureka*.

'Don't you find yourself going—I don't know—a bit stir-crazy here?'

Real amusement lit her aunt's eyes. 'You've

only been here a week. You can't be bored already.'

'Of course not! This place is amazing, beautiful. But I couldn't live here for good. It's so…' *Empty.*

'I enjoy the peace and quiet.'

'But don't you miss catching a movie whenever you want, and seeing your friends—' she went straight for the jugular '—and browsing bookstores?'

'Are you trying to steal my staff, Ms Hartley?'

She swung around to find Jasper striding into the kitchen wearing a pair of brightly coloured board shorts, and both her and her aunt's mouths dropped. Her pulse did a funny little cha-cha. 'I, uh…' She swallowed. 'Well, I'd be fibbing if I said the family wouldn't love it if Aunt Katherine came home.'

'I'll offer you double whatever she's offering, Kate.'

'Very funny.' Katherine's gaze raked up and down his length. Imogen tried not to follow suit. 'But let me see if I have this right. You're going swimming? With Imogen?'

'Not at the same time.' He flicked a glance in Imogen's direction but just as quickly looked away again. 'We'll be taking it in turns to sit with George on the beach.'

Katherine's brows rose. 'But you're going swimming…for fun.'

He stretched his neck first one way and then the other. 'Imogen pointed out, quite rightly, that I have a perfectly good beach sitting on my front doorstep that I hardly seem to use. So I thought I'd…use it.'

Katherine took them in with one glance before giving a smile so blindingly bright Imogen had to blink a couple of times to clear her vision. 'I see Imogen has been working her magic on you.'

Heat flushed up Imogen's neck and into her face. What on earth…?

'I'm glad to see you finally taking a bit of a holiday, Jasper.'

'It's not exactly a holiday. We—'

'The two of you look the picture of youthful holiday fun.'

In her head, she begged her aunt to stop.

'Why don't you leave George with me and go enjoy yourselves?'

The look she sent the two of them was so arch Imogen prayed for the ground to open up and swallow her.

'Wouldn't dream of leaving you with the baby,

Kate,' Jasper said, not looking at Imogen. 'Besides, George loves his daily romp on the beach.'

Without another word, Imogen grabbed her tote and the baby bag and led the way to the front door and outside. She didn't want to meet Jasper's gaze but ignoring him would only make things more awkward.

If that were possible.

She glanced up, but instead of derision or embarrassment she found laughter in those cool grey depths.

A breath whooshed out of her. 'Wow!' Jamming her hat to her head, she pulled it down low on her forehead. 'Just. Wow. That was so not subtle.'

'You can say that again.'

'She used to be the coolest person I knew, but now…' She shook her head.

Spreading the blanket beneath the palm trees in what had become their usual spot on this glorious stretch of beach, she scattered several of George's toys across it, her mind racing. 'It doesn't make sense.'

Jasper lowered George to the blanket. 'Why not?'

She started, realising she'd spoken her concern out loud. 'It's just… I could've sworn when I first arrived that she was warning me off you.'

He eased down onto the blanket too. 'How?'

No way was she telling him that. She adjusted her hat and sat. 'Just telling me to be careful not to bother you. Things like that.'

'She told you I was difficult and demanding, didn't she?'

Damn.

'She told me you were flighty and irresponsible.'

Her mouth fell open. His gaze lowered to her lips for a fraction of a moment, his eyes darkening, before snapping away again. Heat flared in her stomach before charging out to her extremities, making her swallow compulsively. If the man could create that kind of heat in a woman, just from a single smouldering glance, could you imagine—?

Don't imagine.

'You're not flighty and irresponsible any more than I'm difficult and demanding.'

'Exactly.' With a superhuman effort she reined in her pulse. 'So why…?'

'Your aunt is a clever woman. I suspect she's been hoping we'd keep our distance from each other, but George's arrival has put paid to that plan.'

'So why do such an about-face now and literally throw us together?'

He quirked an eyebrow, and she rested back on her hands. 'She *wasn't* trying to throw us together,' she started slowly. 'She was hoping to embarrass us and make us feel so awkward that we'd barely be able to look at each other.'

'That'd be my guess.'

'Why on earth would she do that? I know how well she thinks of you, while I used to be her favourite niece.' But maybe she wasn't any more. She rubbed a hand across her chest. Maybe somewhere along the way she'd lost her aunt's love and respect.

'Imogen, she could think well of me and yet at the same time not think we'd make a good match. She knows the kind of family I come from. I don't blame her for not wanting that for you.'

'Auntie Kay doesn't judge people on their families. She—'

'Go for your swim, Imogen. You've earned it. It doesn't matter why Katherine would prefer not to see us hooking up together, because it's simply not going to happen. It's one of those ridiculous hypothetical scenarios that we needn't concern ourselves with.'

A short sharp jab of pain went through her. It took an effort to keep her voice quiet and measured. 'I don't need warning off, Jasper.'

'That's not what I was doing.'

'Yes, it was.'

He opened his mouth, hesitated and then dragged a hand down his face. 'I'm sorry. I didn't mean to offend you. And it's probably closer to the mark to say I was warning myself off.'

That didn't seem very likely and her disbelief must've shown. He picked George up and held him in front of him—almost as if he were using him as a human shield. 'You're an attractive woman, and you make me laugh. Now, I don't mean to make your aunt sound asexual, but I've known her since I was twelve years old. She practically feels like *my* aunt.'

She frowned, not sure where he was going with this.

'So, in essence, I've spent the last two years on this island without any female company that I'd classify as beguiling or tempting.'

He thought her beguiling and tempting?

'I can't deny that I enjoy your company. I also

appreciate all you've done to help George. I'm just reminding myself not to enjoy it too much.'

He thought her beguiling and tempting?

She moistened her lips, and just for a moment wondered what it'd be like if they did allow themselves to enjoy each other's company *too much.*

She tried to shake the thought off. It was crazy—and crazy-making. She wasn't interested in a fling, and instinct told her he wasn't a fling kind of guy either. Neither of them needed that kind of complication in their lives. He needed to focus on his little nephew—and she wanted to help with that, not become a hindrance.

'You know what?' She rose. 'I might go for that swim now.'

He didn't say anything, just nodded, but she was minutely aware of her body as she untied her sarong—her fingers fumbling with the knot. Jasper thought her beguiling and tempting? The thought awakened something inside her—a sexy siren who wanted to tempt and beguile and make a man lose control—and while she did her best to ignore that siren call, she was unable to keep the sway from her hips as she walked towards the water.

She did her best to lose herself to the push and

pull of the waves, to the invigorating assault of cold water on overheated flesh, and to the thrill of catching perfectly formed waves until she'd worn that siren out—or, at least, had numbed her with cold and exercise. Only then did she emerge back on dry land—out of breath and ready to drop.

Jasper tossed her a towel. 'How was that?'

The siren snapped to attention and Imogen could've wept. She dried off her arms and legs extra vigorously. 'Brilliant. Just give me a moment and you can tag-team me.' She pulled her sea shirt over her head and reached for the dry T-shirt she had in her tote but froze at the hunger that blazed in Jasper's face. Every desire she'd ever had roared to life in an instant.

With a tensing of his jaw, he dragged his gaze away, and, giving herself a mental slap, she scrambled into her dry shirt, wound her sarong back around her waist—not bothering to tie it, knowing her fingers wouldn't work—and knelt on the other side of the blanket from him, careful to keep her eyes fixed on George.

'Your turn!' Her voice emerged too loud and the brightness she injected into it jarred. She'd meant to physically tag him—slap her hand to his—but she changed her mind. One touch and he'd realise she was burning up.

Blowing out a breath, she smiled at George, picked up his teddy bear and danced it along the blanket. 'Water's great once you get in.'

Jasper shot to his feet as if he couldn't wait to be away from her, and she was really careful to keep her gaze from him as he shucked off his shirt, but couldn't resist glancing behind her as he jogged straight into the water without breaking stride, the shock of the cold barely seeming to register.

'Oh, my, George,' she murmured, pushing his toy train towards him and fanning her face. 'Your uncle is hot, hot, hot.'

But off-limits. Definitely off-limits.

Her employer swam for a good twenty minutes.

He's your boss. Don't forget he's your boss.

'Water's pretty damn fine, right?' she said, doing her best to look unaffected by the perfect line of his chest when he stood by the blanket again. The way the towel rubbed across defined pecs and honed abs made her mouth dry.

'Imogen, it's freezing!'

He dragged that towel over his hair before pulling his shirt back on and hiding all of that gloriously masculine muscularity.

That was a good thing.

He sent her a grin and she was relieved to see the strain had faded from his face. It helped ease the tension that had her wound up tight.

'But I know what you mean. I forgot how invigorating that could be.' He spread his towel out beside the blanket and collapsed onto it. 'Did you and young George here have fun?' He tweaked his nephew's toes.

'I had a good think while you were swimming.' Was it her imagination or did he tense at her words? 'About Aunt Katherine,' she added quickly. She didn't want him thinking she was referring to anything else. 'I'm worried about her.'

He sat up, giving her his full attention. 'Why?'

'She told us all back home that she couldn't get the time off at Christmas, that she was needed here on Tesoura. I know that you're not going to give me an answer to this, but I'm starting to suspect that you did give her the time off, and she simply chose not to spend it with us.'

He watched her carefully but didn't say anything.

'She's been avoiding me since I arrived. During the day it's all work, work, work, and at night she tells me she has to get the household accounts into order for your accountant.'

She was doing what?

That was an outright lie. Not that Jasper could say as much to Imogen.

'I think the real reason she's trying to keep us apart is so we don't start comparing notes, realise there *is* something wrong and put our heads together to try and figure out what it is.'

That made a disturbing amount of sense. He knew at least one thing that was troubling Katherine. But was there anything else?

Shame hit him. He hadn't been paying attention. He'd been far too focussed on... He swallowed. He'd been too focussed on himself. Misfortune made some people more empathetic. He, though, had become more self-absorbed.

Look at the way he'd immediately jumped to the conclusion that Emily had sent George to him as part of an elaborate plan of revenge. It still might be, but that didn't change the fact that it shouldn't have been his first concern.

'Jasper, I have a feeling you know more about this than you're letting on.' She stared at him for several long seconds. 'Relax, I'm not going to ask you outright. I understand you have a duty as Katherine's employer and friend to keep her confidences.'

He let out a careful breath.

'But I am going to ask you if I should be as worried as I am.'

His gut clenched at the anxiety reflected in her hazel eyes, at the way her teeth worried her bottom lip. He wanted to ease her mind. He'd do just about anything to make her smile again. But he couldn't lie to her. 'I don't think you should be as worried as you are.'

She let out a long breath and closed her eyes. 'Thank you.'

'But I'm not a hundred per cent sure.'

Her eyes sprang open.

'Would it help if I had a word with your aunt?' He could at least urge Kate to confide in her niece.

She nodded without hesitating. 'Thank you.'

Jasper didn't approach Kate until after dinner, after he'd put George down for the night. Only then did he set his feet in the direction of the kitchen and Katherine's domain, but raised voices had him halting short of the doorway.

'For heaven's sake, Imogen, for the last time

nothing is wrong! I'm getting tired of you harping on the subject.'

'But I'm worried about you.'

'That doesn't give you the right to pester me or pry into my personal life.'

What the...?

'Pry? I haven't pried.' Imogen's incredulity mirrored his own. 'Auntie Kay, we're family. I know Mum's worried about you too, and—'

'While *I* know your mother sent you here to try and pressure me to return home. She's always known how to play the guilt card, but I'm not falling for it this time.'

'That's not fair!'

'It's more than fair. And you coming here as her proxy... It disappoints me, Imogen. I thought better of you.'

'What on earth are you talking about? I—'

'Enough! Yes, your mother and I have had a falling-out, but it's not your place to make me feel guilty about that or to play go-between. I have the right to live my life as I see fit. You're here to work—end of story. I'd appreciate it if you did that without interfering in my personal life.'

Jasper's head reared back. He'd never heard Katherine use that tone before, and he moved forward without thinking, aware of how gutted Imogen must be, and then had to take a step back when Imogen pushed past him with her head down. But that didn't prevent him from recognising the devastation on her face or the betraying sheen in her eyes.

A moment later the front door slammed. He wanted to go after her, make sure she was all right.

He shot into the kitchen and glimpsed Katherine's troubled expression before she quickly masked it again. She wiped the kitchen counters down vigorously. 'Did you want something, Jasper?'

He didn't bother pussyfooting around. 'That seemed unnecessarily harsh.'

'I don't appreciate Gloria's tactics.'

Gloria was her sister—Imogen's mother. 'Imogen isn't Gloria.'

'But she's acting as Gloria's envoy.'

He considered the charge. It didn't add up, not after their conversation earlier on the beach. 'Are you sure about that? Because I'm not.'

Katherine's eyes flew to his. She straightened, setting the dishcloth in the sink. 'What other explanation is there? Why else would Immy be here?'

'For all the reasons she's stated—that she's between jobs, that she wanted to see a little more of the world, that she wanted to spend some time with her favourite aunt.'

'But she keeps asking annoying questions and saying she's worried about me, and—'

'Because she *is* worried. I know that for a fact. Look at it from her perspective. She's come all this way to see you—it's obvious that she adores you—and you're refusing to spend any time with her. And you're using the lamest excuses to avoid her. Now *I* know why you're busy, and *I* know why you're worried, but Imogen doesn't have a clue. And neither does Gloria.'

She pressed a hand to her forehead.

'Is it possible her mother didn't tell her about your argument?'

She blew out a breath. 'Yes.'

'So…?'

'So I'll apologise when she returns and smooth things over.'

'Why don't you tell her the truth? She'll be thrilled for you.'

'Because that will simply give her mother another weapon to use against me. She'll say I don't need an outside job to support myself any more, and that I can just as easily move back home and write there.'

'You can ask Imogen not to tell her.'

'That doesn't seem fair—asking Imogen to keep secrets from her mother.'

'She's a grown-up, Kate. I suspect there are lots of things she doesn't tell her mother.' He hesitated. 'Is there anything other than the book that's bothering you? Because I can—'

'Of course not!'

Her reply came too quickly. Unease circled through him, though he couldn't explain why.

'I can see, however, that you're worried about Immy.'

His shoulders went tight. He didn't like being so easy to read.

'Why don't you go after her and make sure she's okay? Let her know I'm sorry and fill her in on my secret. It's been exhausting to keep it and I'll be glad for her to know the truth.'

'Wouldn't you prefer to do that yourself?'

She shook her head. 'Off you go.' She shooed him out of the kitchen. 'I'll keep an eye on the baby.'

He found Imogen walking along the beach, her hands shoved into the pockets of her shorts and her shoulders hunched. The water lapped at her toes, but she barely seemed aware of it. He moved in next to her, and they walked in silence for a bit. The faintest blush of mauve lingered in the sky to the west as the last of the day's light faded.

'Did you hear all of my exchange with Aunt Katherine?'

She didn't look at him, just kept her eyes trained straight ahead. 'I heard enough to get the general gist.'

A huge golden moon hung low on the horizon, casting a path of dancing light on the water and turning the sand silver except for where the silhouettes of the palm trees made dark shadows. 'I didn't know that she and my mother had fallen out.'

'A fact that occurred to her only after you left.'

She stopped then, her eyes searching his face. The hurt mirrored inside them made his heart burn. 'Really? Or are you just trying to make me feel better?'

He crossed his heart.

Her gaze raked across his face again before something inside her seemed to relax. 'And I'm guessing she perhaps reached that conclusion with a little gentle persuasion from you?'

He didn't answer and she started walking again.

'She is sorry, you know?' he ventured.

She nodded, but still didn't speak. He touched her arm to make her halt. The silk of her skin an invitation hard to resist. 'I saw how upset you were when you left the house, Imogen. I...' He didn't know what it was he wanted to say—that he was worried about her, or that he was sorry she'd argued with her aunt, or that he thought her the most beautiful woman he'd ever laid eyes on?

He tried to dismiss that last thought to some dusty dungeon of his mind. It was just the moonlight talking.

'It's sweet of you to worry about me, Jasper, but I'm fine. To be perfectly honest I'm a bit cranky with both of them for turning me into piggy in the middle.'

She stared out to sea, her hands on her hips. 'Do you know what they fell out about?'

He stared into the dark waves. 'All she said is that she was tired of Gloria pressuring her to return home for good.'

'They've always been chalk and cheese, you know? Mum's the extrovert who's super social while Katherine's the one who has always relished peace and quiet. Mum's also seven years older and still sees Katherine as her little sister who needs brisking up.' She wrinkled her nose. 'It makes her bossy. I don't blame Katherine for getting her nose out of joint and telling Mum to pull her head in.'

'But?'

She shrugged. 'Despite all that, they're really close. I mean, they bicker, but it really rocked everyone when Katherine didn't come home for Christmas. It sent Mum into one of her panics. She was convinced something was wrong.'

And she'd infected her daughter with her own anxiety. 'About Christmas...'

She glanced at him. 'What about it?'

'Your aunt does have something on her mind, and she's given me permission to share it with you.'

She turned to face him fully and it made him hyper-aware of the warm breeze brushing against his calves and the lazy, languid elegance of the nearby palm trees and the rhythmic sound of the sea.

'Which is?'

He snapped back to attention. 'She wants to keep it just between us for the time being. So if you have a problem keeping things from your mother...'

Her eyebrows rose. 'I'll respect my aunt's confidences.'

This really should be coming from Katherine, but he knew how much the older woman hated fuss of any kind. He sympathised with that. He preferred to avoid the spotlight too. 'Well, the truth of the matter is a couple of years ago your aunt had a novel accepted for publication.'

Imogen stared at him in incomprehension for a moment and then everything inside her seemed to electrify. She straightened, her shoulders shot back and she stared at him with huge eyes. 'She's been writing a book?'

'Well, a series, actually. She's had three books accepted so far and is working on her fourth— pulp fiction.' He grinned because he couldn't help it. 'Imogen, you have to read her stuff. It's so much damn fun. A crazy blend of zombie horror and romance, but it works.'

Her jaw dropped. 'You've read them?' And then she thumped his arm. 'I'm *so* jealous.'

'But now you can read them too.' Warmth radiated from where she'd touched him. He tried to ignore it.

She jumped up and down then, clapping her hands. 'Oh, this is the best news. So exciting.' She stopped bouncing to purse her lips. 'She's been keeping it a secret because she thinks my mother will poke fun at her. Mum's a high school English teacher with a high regard for the classics, but she's not a literary snob. In her spare time she reads...'

'Zombie horror?'

A laugh gurgled out of her and it washed over him, rich and warm. 'Cosy mysteries and family sagas. I bet she'd love Katherine's stuff.' She lifted her chin. 'But you know what? They can sort that out for themselves. I'm not getting involved.'

Good for her.

Her face clouded. 'So that's why she didn't want to come home at Christmas?'

'Not exactly. Her publisher wants her to make significant changes to her latest manuscript before they'll agree to publish it. She's been trying to make those changes and struggling with it big-time.'

Comprehension dawned across her face. 'And that's what she's been doing in the evenings—not working on the household accounts but working on her book.'

He nodded because it was too hard to speak when he was fighting to get air into his lungs. The play of emotions across her face in the moonlight, the bounce of her hair and the vulnerable mobility of her lips all held him spellbound.

'Jasper, thank you. I—'

She broke off as their gazes caught and clung.

CHAPTER SEVEN

JASPER WANTED TO kiss her. She recognised the desire alive in his face. It shimmered like the light on a piece of Thai silk—prisms of luminescence arcing delicately against fragile cloth to form rainbows of luxuriant colour. Her every atom yearned towards him. She didn't just *want* him to kiss her—she *ached* with it.

Hovering between breaths, she waited, but he blinked, and she saw him fight to find the strength to gather his resources and step back.

A protest keened through her, but she understood why he did it. He was her boss. Making a move on her would be dishonourable, even though her employment status in his house fell firmly in the temporary category.

But she could make a move on *him* first, right?

She moistened her bottom lip. His gaze zeroed in on the action, hunger darkening his eyes and making his breathing ragged. The pulse at the base of his throat raced.

Why, yes. Yes, she could.

A thrill raced through her. 'Have you ever seen a more glorious moon?' she whispered, pointing to it though her gaze didn't leave his.

His gaze didn't leave hers either. 'No.'

'I once strolled along the Seine in the moonlight on a warm spring night, and I didn't think there could be a more romantic setting in the world. But I was wrong.'

His nostrils flared. 'You think my island is romantic?'

She nodded. 'Standing here on this beach now with a moon like that—all bright and vibrant—hovering just above the horizon like some kind of jewel, and with a warm breeze playing across my bare skin, that gorgeous perfume I've never smelled before drifting across from the forest and mingling with the scent of the sea...'

His Adam's apple bobbed.

'It feels like magic. And *very* romantic.'

His eyes throbbed into hers.

'I want to kiss you, Jasper.'

'Imogen.' Her name was barely more than a groan wrenched from his throat.

'I won't if you don't want me to.'

He closed his eyes, all the muscles in his jaw bunching.

'You know those moments you wished you'd taken, but you let slip away? And then spend the rest of your life kicking yourself for?'

His gaze returned to hers.

'This feels like one of those moments.'

A slow breath eased out of him, drawing her attention to the strong column of his throat and down to broad shoulders that made her mouth dry.

She forced her gaze back to his, not bothering to hide her need. 'I know it can't be anything more than a kiss. I'm not usually impulsive like this. I'm not into flings. But once I leave your gorgeous island, I'm starting a new phase of my life. This might be my last chance...'

He edged closer. 'To?'

'To seize the perfect moment—to live in it—without worrying about the consequences. To revel in a moment out of time one last time.'

His face gentled. 'A moment out of time?'

'A moment that, even when we're old and grey, will still put a smile on our faces whenever we remember it.'

His knuckles brushed across her cheek, firing her every nerve ending with heat and lust. His smile, when it came, made her thighs tremble. 'Then we'd better make it memorable.'

Her pulse started to gallop. She did what she could to get it under control—at least a little—because she didn't want to rush this moment. She wanted to savour it and imprint it on her mind for all time.

Which sounded crazy and overly dramatic, but she didn't care. She was following her gut all the way on this one.

Lifting her hands to touch his face, she revelled in the feel of his day-old growth as it scraped across her palms. He held still, waiting. 'What?' he eventually whispered, and she realised she'd been staring.

'There's something else that makes this moment incredibly romantic.'

'What's that?'

'You,' she murmured. She couldn't believe that she was touching him; that she was going to get to kiss him. 'You're beautiful, Jasper.' She could've chosen any number of words. *Gorgeous. Hot. Sexy.* They all fitted. But the one she'd uttered felt perfect. 'Beautiful inside and out.'

His lips parted as if in shock. His eyes had grown soft. 'Imogen...'

But she was done with talking. She slid her hands around his neck and pulled his head down to hers, reaching up on tiptoe to touch her lips to his.

The spark that ran through her made her tremble, but his hands at her waist held her steady. It gave her the security, and the boldness, to lean farther into him and move her lips across his more firmly. He was an intoxicating mixture of softness and strength, and kissing him was as invigorating as swimming in wild surf. It electrified her. And it must've electrified him too because it was as if their blood started racing at the same speed and to the same beat; their mouths opened at the same time and their tongues tangled as they tried to devour each other.

Wind roared in her ears, blocking out the sound of the surf. One of his hands pressed against the small of her back, urging her closer. The other flattened between her shoulder blades, hauling her against him. Every inch of her from the hips up could feel all of him. She wrapped her arms around his neck and tried to get even closer. The kiss went beyond anything she'd ever experienced. As if together they'd become the sea, sand and sun. As if crashing against each other, washing against each other, and heating each other up was what they were designed for.

She wrapped one leg around his waist to angle

her pelvis more firmly against his. One large hand splayed beneath her thigh to hold it in place, and with a guttural groan he thrust against her. She threw her head back with a cry of pure need, arching into him.

She didn't know who stilled first. The way it felt—as if the moon had cast some spell on them and had cosmically attuned them to each other—they might've stopped at exactly the same moment. They stared into each other's stunned eyes. At least, she expected she must look as shell-shocked as him. She felt as if she were in a snow globe and someone had just shaken it—and the landscape of her life would never settle into the exact same contours again.

He let go of her leg. She lowered it to the ground.

He unwrapped his arm from her waist. She removed her hands from his shoulders.

She touched her fingers to her lips. He swallowed. 'Did I hurt you?'

She shook her head. 'No, but...wow.' Heat continued to spark across her skin like a tropical storm. 'I mean...wow!'

He nodded.

'No.' She shook her head. 'I mean a real *wow.*'

'Imogen—'

'I really wasn't expecting *that*.' She knew she was babbling but couldn't stop. 'I thought it was going to be some really sweet kiss that…' She shook her head at his pulsing, dark-eyed silence. 'But that wasn't *sweet*. I was ready to tear your clothes off and do things to you and with you that I've never—'

He reached out and pressed his fingers to her mouth with a low curse that made her close her eyes. Eventually she managed a nod. 'Sorry. Too much information.'

'For the record, I wasn't expecting things to get so intense so quickly either.' His hands clenched. 'I've been on this island too damn long.'

She gulped in air. 'Oh, no, you don't. You're not taking *all* the credit for that. It had just as much to do with me as it did with you. And I don't care what stupid excuses you want to make, but together we…*rock*.'

Bracing his hands on his knees, he huffed out a laugh. 'That's one way of putting it.' He straightened and met her gaze. 'But we both know it can't go beyond that, right?'

'I know.' She scratched both hands back through her hair and then frowned. She bit her lip and stuck out a hip. 'Why not?'

Her question slipped out without her meaning it to. Maybe the kiss had short-circuited her thought processes. His face grew grim and for a moment she thought he might revert to the wounded bear she'd met when she'd first arrived here, that he'd turn around and stalk off without another word. But then his face gentled again and he almost smiled. 'Because you're not romantically impulsive?'

And neither was he?

'You don't do flings.'

And he wasn't offering anything more.

Got it.

'You're only in Tesoura for a short time. You have big plans for your life. Exciting plans.'

She did. And she'd never be so foolish as to sacrifice those plans for a love affair. 'That's right.' She slapped a hand to her forehead. 'I remember now.' She eyed him carefully. 'And you have no plans to leave Tesoura?'

'None. This is my home now.'

She pulled in a breath. 'You're right. This can't go beyond that kiss. Sorry—' she shot him what she really hoped was a smile '—the oxygen is finally reaching my brain again.'

He laughed, and she wished she couldn't feel its rumble all the way to the centre of her being.

'There are other reasons too, Imogen. Many

reasons. I'm going to tell you a story so you can understand what I mean.'

A story?

He pointed at the moon, and she turned to look. 'It still looks amazing,' he said.

But not as amazing as it had a moment ago. As it had moved farther into the sky, it had diminished in both size and colour. It looked neither as big nor as vividly yellow, as if it had lost some of its heat and energy.

Jasper surprised her when he moved behind and wrapped an arm about her shoulders and drew her back against him. She didn't resist, just let his warmth surround her. It was a protective gesture, a gesture of camaraderie, and it was kind. He didn't want her to feel alone, and he didn't want her to feel rejected.

The moon blurred and her throat ached.

'Do you remember asking what had happened to me?'

She nodded, not trusting herself to speak.

'I think if I tell you that story, you'll understand—and agree—that it's better for me to be on my own.'

She frowned out at the dark water, lifting a hand to squeeze his forearm in a show of silent support. She couldn't see how she was ever going to agree that he should be *on his own*. Not forever. She got the fact that he might not want to be with her, but this self-imposed exile? He deserved better than that.

'I've already told you my father was physically abusive. He had a big leather belt that he wielded with great...authority. When he wasn't using his fists.'

She flinched, and his arm tightened about her.

'My mother copped most of his anger, though she's spent her entire life trying to placate him. I stepped in when I could...when doors weren't locked.'

She closed her eyes, but the image of the young boy he must've been was burned onto the insides of her eyelids. She forced her eyes open again. 'And then *you* copped it.' He didn't say anything. He didn't need to. 'Emily?'

'Mum and I did our best to protect her. She's a couple of years older than me, but she's always been a tiny little thing.'

Her heart burned.

'They say history never repeats, but they're wrong. In Emily's case it did. I never really liked Aaron all that much—thought him kind of smarmy—but I figured Emily was better off with him than at home where Dad was liable to lash out without warning. I'm guessing that's what she thought too.'

If Emily had never had a strong female role model like Imogen, then...then she'd have never really stood a chance.

'I dropped in on Em and Aaron unexpectedly one evening. I could hear raised voices upstairs, so I let myself in and followed the ruckus to its source. Where I saw Aaron backhand my sister. I saw red.'

'What happened?'

'I punched him, but evidently not hard enough because he got up and came at me. Emily was screaming at us to stop.' He paused. 'He charged. I sidestepped. Don't get me wrong, I had every intention of beating the living daylights out of him, but not in front of Emily. She'd been traumatised enough.'

He went so still she started to worry. She wrapped both her hands around his forearm and held on tight, pressed back against him, wanting him to know that he wasn't alone.

A breath shuddered out of him. 'His momentum sent him crashing across the landing and down the stairs.'

She gave a slow nod. It evidently hadn't killed the guy as he was still making Emily's life a misery… 'I'm finding it hard to feel any sympathy for him.'

A low chuckle broke from his throat, disturbing the hair near her ear and making her break out in gooseflesh. 'I can't say I felt too much of that at the time either. He broke his leg badly in two places. He walks with a limp and still needs a stick to get around. He's lucky to not be in a wheelchair apparently.'

She had a feeling he was lucky Jasper hadn't managed to get his hands on him good and proper.

'He accused me of assault. I was charged and a trial date was set.'

All Aunt Katherine had told her earlier came back now. She spun in his arms. 'But it didn't go to court.'

He stepped away and she immediately missed his warmth. His laugh held a bitter edge. 'He knew his charges would never stick. His fall down the stairs was an accident of his own making, not mine.'

So he'd dropped them, but… 'Why didn't Emily break free of him when she had the chance?'

This time his laugh held even more bitterness. 'Believe me, I wish I knew. I tried to get her to leave him.'

Her heart pounded so hard her chest hurt. 'But?'

'She told me she still loved him. She said he'd only forgotten himself that once, had only hit her that one time, and that it had been her fault for goading him into it.'

Imogen covered her face with her hands.

'She told me her relationship with Aaron was none of my business, that she hated me for what I'd done.'

She pulled her hands away to stare at him in disbelief. She felt suddenly and utterly exhausted. He must feel at least a hundred times worse.

'She said she'd never forgive me for hurting Aaron, and that she never wanted to see me again.'

And he'd not heard from her until last week? 'Your parents?'

'They took Aaron's side. My father and Aaron were always as thick as thieves, and my father had been looking for an excuse to sever all ties with me for years. He seized this one when it came along, lost no time in telling the tabloids my temper had always been a problem.'

'What an absolute pig of a man!'

'He forbade my mother from having any contact with me.'

It wasn't her place, she knew that, but she was angry with his mother too—*livid*. She pressed her lips together as hard as she could for a moment before releasing them. 'Do you miss them?'

'I don't miss my father.' He glanced at her with shadowed eyes. 'I have no love left in me for him. He destroyed that a long time ago. But my mother and sister…'

He missed them. She could see it. He'd banished himself to this island in despair because he hadn't been able to save them.

'I call my mother twice a year. I ask her the same questions. Can I come and get you? Is there anything I can do to help you get away from him?'

He was keeping the lines of communication open. Letting her know she had an escape route if she needed it. Imogen wanted to hug him.

'She refuses every single time. She tells me she likes her life.' He was quiet for a moment. 'I made her memorise my phone number in case she ever needs to call.' He shook his head. 'Emily still refuses to speak to me.'

For the last two years he'd been on his own, with no one to talk to about any of this. It had to have been festering away inside him like poison. She wanted to cry for him. 'Jasper, I'm so sorry.'

He nodded. With what looked like a concerted effort, he pushed his shoulders back and smiled. The sadness in his eyes, though, pierced her soul. 'So you can see why I think it best that I remain on my own.'

She didn't bother fighting her frown. 'Actually, I'm afraid I don't.'

His jaw went slack. 'Imogen—' he leaned towards her '—my family is complicated…ugly.'

'So what? It's not who you are. If a woman cared about you, she wouldn't give two hoots about your complicated family. She'd care about you—that's what would matter. I'm sorry, Jasper, but I don't get that reasoning at all.'

Jasper pinched the bridge of his nose, tried to ignore the way his heart leapt at her words. 'I missed out one important thread in my story.'

He called it a story because he desperately wanted to put some distance between it and him. But it didn't seem to be working.

Imogen pressed her hands to her abdomen as if she were fighting nausea. 'There's more?'

'I had a fiancée.' He forced himself to straighten. 'It wasn't public knowledge—we hadn't announced it yet. Bronwyn was, and still is, a cellist with the Sydney Symphony Orchestra. My father threatened her career—told her he'd have her dismissed from the orchestra—if she didn't break things off with me.'

Bronwyn's betrayal was still a raw ugly wound, though he'd never blamed her for her decision to walk away from him—not in the least. His father had threatened her career, her livelihood… her dream. 'He told her he'd see to it that she'd never play again.'

'So…she broke up with you?'

'I don't hold her responsible for that.'

Her eyes filled and his throat thickened. 'I can see that. Though, I'm not sure I'd have been so forgiving in your place.'

Imogen thought she'd act differently, but she didn't know Keith Coleman. She didn't understand how dangerous he could be. And Jasper had no intention of her ever finding out.

'*That's* why I need to be on my own, Imogen. *That's* why I can't have any ties. My father will go after the woman I love and do whatever he can to destroy her.'

'So you're not even prepared to risk it? Even if this hypothetical woman you love—and who loves you—not only has her own resources to rely on, but yours as well?' She leaned towards him. 'You're a wealthy man. That gives you a measure of power and protection.'

'It's not worth the risk. We're not just talking about someone's livelihood here, but their dreams—things they've been working towards their entire lives.' He could never ask a woman to give that up for him. 'My father has political power. His connections include key industry and business figures. He wields his influence with about as much care—and as much gusto—as George does his toy train. I will never put a woman in a position where she could be hurt by him.'

'Then your father has won. You're letting him win.'

Her words had a resonance that sounded through him. Maybe she was right, but at least he could prevent his father from hurting another woman.

'No woman needs that hassle in her life. It's not a war she should be forced to fight. It wouldn't be fair. I refuse to be the catalyst for that kind of damage. It wouldn't be fair,' he repeated, before drawing himself up. 'Have you heard the mantra "do no harm"?'

She stared out at the water for three beats and then turned back with a nod.

He slapped a hand to his chest and met her gaze. She pulled in a breath as if she understood everything he was trying to say. For some reason that only made his heart burn harder.

'Life isn't fair, Jasper. No matter what you do, life isn't fair. It's not fair that you have such a father. It's not fair that a jerk of an ex-boyfriend of mine calls me stupid. It's not fair that my mother—'

He jerked to attention. 'Your mother?'

She shrugged. 'It wasn't fair that she and my aunt had to watch my grandmother die from breast cancer.'

Some sixth sense told him it wasn't what she'd originally meant to say. She turned on him, though, before he could challenge her. 'The thing is, whatever you do—you're not going to be able to protect everyone from everything. And you don't know what unforeseen consequences your attempts to keep everyone safe—your attempts to *do no harm*—could have either.'

'What are you talking about?' The decision he'd made was the right one, damn it.

'The day after you'd broken up with her, Bronwyn could've just as easily tripped and fractured a wrist. Hey presto, she can no longer play in the orchestra. That stuff happens all the time. But if you'd still been together and you'd been walking beside her, you might've caught her. And hey presto, no broken wrist.'

He rolled his eyes. 'You're being ridiculous. You're creating imaginary scenarios that may or may not happen and—'

'So are you!'

His head rocked back. He felt as if she'd slapped him.

'You're saying *if* you let a woman close, and *if* your father finds out about it then he *might* threaten her in some way. And *if* that happens, you're saying she's going to walk away from you…and *if* she doesn't then she's going to get hurt because you and her don't have the power to fight your father.'

His teeth ground together.

'That's a lot of *ifs* and *mights*, Jasper.'

He counted to ten. 'You haven't lived the life I've lived. And you don't know my father the way I do. This is no longer up for discussion.'

'But—'

'Look, I know that kiss was spectacular. But spectacular kisses don't necessarily lead to spectacular relationships.'

She drew herself up to her full height, which meant she reached the top of his nose. 'This isn't about me.'

'Are you sure?' He knew it wasn't, but he asked the question to deliberately anger her, to distance and alienate her. It'd be much better that she think him a jerk than for his father to—

His hands clenched. He would *not* let his father hurt her. He would not allow that man to dim this woman's fire or to crush her dreams.

Her soft laugh jerked him back. 'You're being a deliberate jackass now.'

His jaw clenched before he forced it to relax again. 'We really need you to work on that subservience thing.'

'You're being a deliberate jackass, *sir.*'

He had to cover his mouth to hide a smile.

She turned and started back along the beach in the direction of the house. He fell into step beside her, doing his best to not breathe in the notes of vanilla and citrus that seemed to be a part of her. Water foamed up suddenly around her ankles, making her smile. It was such a simple pleasure, and in that instant he felt bad for being, as she'd put it, a jackass.

'That kiss, Imogen...'

Was it his imagination or did she stiffen? 'Hmm...?'

'You're right, you know? It's not the kind of kiss one forgets.'

'Burned on my brain,' she agreed.

He envied her that cheerful candour. 'And when I'm old and grey and I remember it, it's going to make me smile. Every single time.'

'Me too.'

She sent him a smile full of warmth, but a new distance lurked at its edges, a distance he'd created, and his heart protested. A defiant part of him wanted to smash the barriers he'd forced her to put into place. But to what end? So he could hurt her more?

He clenched his hands. Sometimes spectacular kisses did lead to spectacular relationships, but mostly they didn't. He and Imogen didn't have a relationship—not in that sense—and they weren't going to. A man who couldn't find a way to protect his own mother and sister didn't deserve love and romance. His chest burned. He wasn't worthy of a woman like Imogen.

He pulled in a breath and steeled himself. He couldn't kiss Imogen again. He *had* to resist.

CHAPTER EIGHT

IMOGEN HAD HEARD about raging emotions—
had read about them in books, and had even experienced them a time or two, but not like this.
She felt as if she were being battered by cyclonic
winds and stinging rain. A part of her wanted to
seek shelter, to lick wounds that had started to
throb with a nagging persistence that made her
temples ache.

Another part of her wanted to seize Jasper and
kiss him again, to drag him into the maelstrom
with her. If he kissed her back it would make all
those aches go away. She knew that on a primal
level.

But if he didn't kiss her back…

She pulled in a breath and swallowed. If he
didn't kiss her back it'd make everything hurt
twice as much. And she couldn't kiss him again.
Not after he'd told her he didn't want her to.

When they reached the edge of his garden,
she halted and closed her eyes. 'That birdcall is

lovely,' she said on the pretence of listening to something rather than calling attention to the effort she was making to calm the storm raging inside her.

She needed to compose herself before she spoke to her aunt.

She could feel Jasper's eyes on her, assessing her, so she did what she could to smooth out her face. 'Do you know what it is?'

She opened her eyes to find him shaking his head. She resisted the urge to point out that he demonstrated a remarkable lack of interest in his idyllic island retreat—the place he now apparently called home. She'd bet a therapist would have something insightful to say about that.

She pressed her lips together to stop herself from playing therapist.

He opened the front door and ushered her ahead of him. She refused to notice the warm spicy scent of him—or his beguiling heat—as she slipped past.

Don't think about Jasper. Focus on Aunt Katherine.

Katherine and George were in the living room, and, with the windows dark now from the night, the room reminded Imogen even more of a ship. George, looking sleepy on his blanket on the floor, cuddled his toy rabbit with its super-long ears. Katherine, looking worried, leapt up from the sofa the moment they entered.

'Imogen, honey, I'm sorry about earlier,' she started at the same time Imogen spoke.

'You've written a book!'

And then they both laughed and hugged.

'I shouldn't have said what I did,' Katherine said, pulling Imogen down to the sofa beside her.

George saw his uncle and let go of his soft toy to kick his legs and lift his arms to be picked up. With a smile that caught at her stupid, susceptible heart, Jasper lifted him and cradled him against his shoulder. She now knew how strong those arms were, how broad and solid those shoulders.

'I should've known Gloria hadn't told you about our tiff.'

Imogen hauled herself back, studiously averting her gaze from man and baby.

'My only excuse is that I've not been sleeping well and…'

Imogen reached for her aunt's hand. 'Jasper tells me you're having trouble with your latest book.'

'It's a hot mess, but I think I'm finally starting to make progress.'

Katherine's smile didn't quite reach her eyes, so Imogen didn't believe her, and while she didn't want to add to her aunt's stress, she didn't want to keep secrets from her any longer either. 'I didn't know about your falling-out with Mum, Auntie Kay, but there is something you probably should know.'

Katherine stared at her—and so did Jasper as he lowered himself into the armchair opposite. She could feel his attention like a laser beam and she really, *really* wished she could just not be aware of it…not be aware of *him*.

Katherine seized Imogen's shoulders, her face losing all colour. 'Immy, please tell me she doesn't have breast cancer.'

It hit her then how much her grandmother's death had affected the two sisters. 'I promise you, she doesn't have breast cancer.'

Katherine sagged. 'You frightened me out of my wits.'

'I'm sorry, I didn't mean to. There is an issue, but it's not as serious as cancer. Back in November Mum found out she has macular degeneration.'

Katherine stared at her. 'She's going blind?'

Imogen's eyes filled and she nodded. 'She has

time yet. They can delay it by giving her injections into her eyes, but eventually...'

'Why didn't she tell me?'

'She was going to tell you in person at Christmas.'

'But I didn't come home.' Katherine tapped a finger against her mouth. 'So that's why she's been so passive-aggressive recently and telling me that my being so far away isn't fair to your grandfather.'

'You know what she's like. She's focussing all of her worry on who's going to look after Granddad if she's blind.'

Katherine stiffened, and then without warning burst into tears. Imogen wrapped an arm about her shoulders, her throat thickening. 'She's going to be fine, Auntie Kay, I promise you. Like I said, there's time. It could be years before her eyesight becomes truly bad. There's time for everyone to adjust, to put strategies into place. And there's no need for you to come home—not for good. Dad and I can look after Granddad—'

'Darling girl, that's not your job.' Katherine lifted her head and wiped her eyes. 'The thing is...'

Katherine's expression had ice fist-bumping

down Imogen's spine. Jasper leaned towards them. 'What is the thing?' she croaked.

'Just before Christmas, I found a lump in my breast.'

Imogen's hand flew to her mouth. Her heart pounded so hard it was nearly impossible to breathe. 'You spent the holidays getting tests?'

Oh, please, don't let Auntie Kay have cancer, please—

Katherine's gaze dropped. 'No.'

No? But… Grandma had *died* of breast cancer. Katherine had seen the effects, had—

'I went to a little village on the mainland and worked on my book. And waited for the lump to go away.'

Her mouth went dry. 'Auntie Kay…'

Jasper shot to his feet, his face set, though his eyes blazed. He still held the baby against his shoulder as if it were the most precious thing in the world—cradling him there as if he wanted to protect him from all hurt.

Katherine glanced from one to the other. 'I meant to.' Her bottom lip trembled. 'But I was afraid. I didn't realise that's the way I'd react. I couldn't face the thought of…' She covered her face briefly. 'But if I do have breast cancer and if I die and if Gloria goes blind then…who will look after your grandfather? Your uncles won't know what to do. And I—'

'Kate.' The quiet authority in Jasper's voice had them both turning to him. 'That's an awful lot of ifs on very little evidence.'

Had he meant to repeat the words she'd said to him earlier?

His brows drew down over his eyes. 'Why didn't you tell me?'

'We don't talk about personal matters, Jasper.'

'But this is your health!'

'I was hoping it'd go away. I know that probably sounds stupid to you both, but—'

'No,' Imogen said. 'I get it. But, Auntie Kay, we have to get you examined.'

Katherine hesitated and then nodded. 'I'll make an appointment tomorrow.'

Jasper widened his stance. He looked suddenly immovable. 'We can do better than that. I'll organise a seaplane for first thing in the morning, and I'll have you seen by a team of Brazil's best medical professionals ASAP.'

Katherine thrust out her jaw. 'Don't come over all high-handed with me, Jasper. You can't force me into anything I don't want and—'

'Kate, I would never force you into anything against your will. *Never.*'

Jasper wasn't his father. She could see now how he'd modelled himself to become the exact opposite—the protector rather than the abuser. She wanted to leap up and hug him—for his kindness to Katherine, but also for all the constant restrictions he placed on himself, for the sacrifices he made without asking for anything in return. A man like Jasper deserved to be surrounded by family and love.

The fight drained out of her aunt. 'I know. I'm sorry. It's just that things are going to start moving so quickly now and it feels as if everything will start spinning out of my control.'

Imogen seized her hand. 'As soon as we have answers, it'll stop the spinning.' She tightened her grip. 'You know that in the majority of cases lumps are benign.'

'But what if it's not? With my history…'

Fear clutched at Imogen's heart.

'We take it one step at a time,' Jasper interspersed calmly. 'If it isn't benign, then we'll make a plan. You'll take a deep breath and consider all your options. We'll find a way forward, Kate. You're healthy and still young. I promise, you won't be on your own.'

Katherine pulled in a deep breath and nodded. Imogen could see her mentally steel herself to face whatever the future had in store. Jasper fumbled with his phone and Imogen leapt to take the baby.

'He was fussing earlier,' Katherine murmured, 'so I brought him downstairs. But he seems to have settled again now.'

'I'll go put him down.'

It took her next to no time to put the sleepy baby to bed. She started back towards the living room but halted in the shadows at the top of the stairs when her aunt said, 'Jasper, I can't afford the kind of treatment you're talking about.'

Jasper's head lifted from where he furiously texted on his phone. 'Healthcare benefits were part of your employment package.'

Katherine snorted, and Imogen didn't blame her. The man was a *terrible* liar.

He dragged a hand down his face. 'Okay, I have a lot of money. It's just sitting there doing nothing. Please let me do this for you. Let me do something good with it.'

The room blurred, and Imogen's throat thickened.

'You've been a rock—one of the few stable elements in my life. You mean a lot to me. You're like…family.' He gave a half laugh. 'The family

I wished I had. Not the messed-up excuse that I got. Please let me do this one thing for you.'

'You can't refuse that, Auntie Kay.' The words burst from Imogen as she flew down the stairs. *Accept his offer*, she wanted to yell. It had been made with a good and pure intent.

'Immy's right. I can't refuse you when you put it like that. Thank you, Jasper. I'm grateful... and touched.'

Katherine rose and gave him a hug. Her eyes were wet when she released him several moments later and his were suspiciously bright at well.

'So you'll be ready to leave at six in the morning?'

Katherine nodded.

Imogen eased forward. 'Can I help with anything?' She'd sit up all night and hold her aunt's hand if it'd help.

'Thank you, Immy, but no. I'm going to pack a few things and then do some breathing exercises. A bit of quiet now is what I need.'

She watched her aunt leave the room before swinging to Jasper. 'Thank you. A million times, thank you.'

'It's nothing.'

'It's everything! To know we'll have an answer one way or another soon…' Didn't he know what a big thing that was? 'Knowing will help. I know she's been hiding from it, and I know she's afraid.' Imogen was terrified so it must be a thousand times worse for her aunt. 'But getting an answer—knowing—is good. And you're making sure that happens as soon as possible.'

'It's the least I can do.'

It was more than most would've done. She didn't say as much, though. It was taking all her strength and concentration not to get caught up in the clear grey of his eyes and the beguiling breadth of his shoulders.

'You'll be okay here on your own for a couple of days with George while Katherine and I go to the mainland?'

She wished she could go too but she swallowed and nodded. 'Of course. Eduardo's here if I need help with anything.' She lifted her chin. She wasn't adding to the expense or the hassle of the trip. She could talk to her aunt every day on the phone.

Those eyes didn't leave her face. 'You want to be with your aunt.'

It was a statement, not a question. 'I wouldn't be human if I didn't want that. But it's neither here nor there. You're…'

She trailed off when he punched a number into his phone and lifted it to his ear. 'Antonio, is there room for another two passengers—one adult and one baby?'

Imogen's heart thumped.

'Excellent. Thank you.'

'It's really not necessary,' she whispered.

'Your aunt will be happier if you're with her. And it's your aunt we need to think about.'

'I swear to God you just became my new favourite person, Jasper.'

Just for a moment his eyes crinkled. And she wanted to hug him so badly things inside her hurt. As if he read that thought on her face, he took a step back. 'Pack light. One small bag. Plan for a two-night stay. If we need anything else, we can buy it on the mainland. I'd better finish making the arrangements and pack for me and George.'

She watched him leave. 'Goodnight, Jasper,' she murmured once he'd disappeared from view.

Her new favourite person? She swallowed. She hadn't been joking.

She was in trouble. Big trouble.

Jasper had made arrangements for the seaplane to take them to the port of Santos—an hour away—and from there a limousine took them to São Paulo. He'd ordered Evan to find him the best darn medical facility in the city. His assistant had gone above and beyond. Not only had he shortlisted five hospitals with excellent reputations, but he'd also managed to book Katherine into one of them for a biopsy that very morning. He didn't know what strings Evan had pulled or how much money it was going to cost, but he didn't care. Kate deserved the absolute best.

He sank into a chair in the hallway outside her door, dropping his head to his hands. Why hadn't he taken better care of Kate? Why hadn't he insisted on taking her and Eduardo to the mainland once a year for medicals?

He'd become unforgivably self-absorbed since arriving on Tesoura. He'd lost a part of himself when Bronwyn, Emily and his mother had turned their backs on him. He'd shut himself off emotionally, fooled himself into thinking that large donations to women's refuges could replace emotion and caring. But he'd been wrong.

The door to Kate's room opened and he straightened. He didn't want either woman to see how worried he was. He needed to be strong for them. Imogen's ashen face as she walked out squeezed his chest tight. He drew her down to the seat beside him. George continued to sleep in blissful ignorance in the nearby stroller. 'Your aunt is in excellent hands.'

'I know. And I'm so grateful to you, Jasper.' She sent him a brave little smile that twisted his insides. 'They're about to take her down for the biopsy, but she wants a word with you before she goes.'

With a nod, he shot to his feet and strode into Kate's room. 'How are you feeling? Is there anything I can get for you?'

'Now that I'm here, I'm feeling remarkably calm.'

He sat on the edge of her bed. 'Is there anything you'd like me to do?'

'Actually, there is.'

He leaned towards her, all attention. 'Name it.'

'I'm going to be busy with tests all day, Jasper. I don't want Imogen fretting any more than she already is. Besides, a hospital waiting room is no place for a baby. I want you to take her out to see the sights—get her mind off things for a while. I don't want to see either one of you until visiting hours this evening.'

'But—'

She raised an eyebrow and he swallowed back his protests. 'I've a novel I wouldn't mind finishing. I have a pen and notepad because a new story idea has come calling, which is far from convenient considering I haven't finished my current one yet but playing around with that will keep me busy. And I have a playlist full of my favourite songs. I've everything I need to keep me calm and occupied.'

He read the subtext. Him and Imogen fussing and hovering would add to her stress—their anxiety would feed hers. He flashed to Imogen's pale face and nodded. Sitting here worrying wouldn't do her any good either. He fished out his phone and brought up a list of current 'things to do' in São Paulo and scanned the offerings. His lips lifted, and he met Kate's gaze. 'Done. Now is there anything I can get or do for you before I whisk Imogen away for the day?'

'I have everything I need, thank you. You've gone above and beyond.'

He rose, hesitated and then leaned across to press a kiss to her cheek. 'We're just a phone call away. If you need us…'

She nodded, blinking hard, and then she rolled her eyes as two orderlies came into the room pushing a wheelchair. 'Honestly, is that necessary? You are aware that I haven't lost the use of my legs?'

Jasper hid a smile. She pointed a finger at him. 'Now, I'm looking forward to being regaled with your adventures later this evening, so don't let me down.'

He saluted and left the room. Imogen glanced up and he forced a cheerfulness he was far from feeling. 'Come on.' He took the stroller and started to wheel it down the hall. 'We've been banished.'

She rose automatically but she didn't move. 'By who?'

He linked an arm though hers and urged her forward. 'Who do you think?'

'Oh, but—'

'Imogen, Kate is going to be busy with tests all day. It's not like we're going to get a chance to see her between those tests or to sit with her.'

'I know. I just… I want to be close in case she needs us.'

'She has both our numbers on speed dial.' He forced himself to release her. Touching her made him…actually it unmade him. 'Do you know what she's looking forward to?'

'What?'

'Us regaling her with our adventures for the day.'

'But—'

'Wondering what we're getting up to is one of the things that will help her get through today.'

She worried at her lip.

'And you know how she hates fuss of any kind.'

She worried harder and he wanted to wrap her in his arms and tell her everything would be all right. Only he didn't know if it would be. Panic tried to let loose inside him, but he reined it in. 'And this isn't a place for a baby.'

She glanced at George and her shoulders slumped. 'Okay, but if you think some cathedral or museum is going to take my mind off what's happening here you have rocks in your head.'

'That sounds like a challenge.' He pushed the stroller into motion again, and her eyes widened at what he expected was the smug expression on his face. 'I'll bet you lunch at an authentic Brazilian eatery that it does.'

Her jaw dropped. 'You're on,' she said with a glare.

Twenty minutes later a taxi set them down at their destination—the museum of contemporary art. Imogen watched the taxi depart. 'Your Portuguese is very good. When did you learn?'

'When I first arrived on Tesoura. It seemed the polite thing to do.'

He'd banished himself to an island and had

learned a language he hardly ever used because he never went anywhere, and he never saw anyone. What kind of sense did that make?

He shook the thought away as she glanced at the building in front of him. 'So this is a…museum.'

'Not just any museum. Here, you take the top and I'll take the bottom.' He gestured to the stroller and together they manoeuvred it up the stairs.

'What's so special about—?'

She broke off when she saw the sign advertising the current exhibition, and he grinned at her expression. 'You mean besides the fact that there's currently a costume exhibition showing here?'

The woman was a dressmaker, a seamstress—she'd worked in Paris and was opening her own sewing school in a couple of months. He figured the one thing in this entire amazing city that had the potential to charm her, to fire her enthusiasm and imagination, was a historic collection of amazing clothes.

She slammed her hands on her hips, and he could see her try to work up some righteous outrage. 'You exploited my weakness for a free lunch?'

'Hey, whatever works.'

She glanced at the sign again. 'Well, it looks as if lunch is definitely on me.' She threaded her arm through his and he had to grit his teeth against the rush of warmth that sped through him. 'C'mon, I can't wait to see this. When Aunt Katherine hears about it, you're going to get the biggest gold star.'

The next two hours flew by. The clothes on display were utterly amazing—everything from indigenous ceremonial robes, intricate Renaissance ball gowns, to costumes used in popular soap operas. There were hats and shoes, underclothes and tools of the trade that meant very little to him. It wasn't the items on display that held his attention, but Imogen's rapt delight. Her explanations of the techniques used and her appreciation for the fine craftsmanship had him transfixed.

'Your sewing school is going to be amazing.'

She stilled but didn't look at him. 'What makes you say that?'

'You have a real passion for all of this. And passion is the thing that makes the difference. People are drawn to it. It gives you the energy and drive to succeed. It means that when you hit a road bump, you'll find a way around it.'

He could almost sense the doubts piling up inside her. 'And you shouldn't let that stupid exboyfriend of yours convince you otherwise.'

She swung to him, her mouth dropping, but then she turned back to the displays and he let the matter drop. Her passion challenged him in ways he hadn't expected. He'd been passionate once—passionate about building his company into a globally recognised brand; passionate about doing all he could to help his mother and sister; passionate about neutralising his father and the harm he did.

He'd let his passion die. And in the process, he'd become a robot. His chest cramped. His passion for life and justice might've died, but it didn't mean he had to become a miserable excuse for a human being.

He shook the thought off and picked up George's tossed bunny for the fifth time. George squealed in joy when Jasper handed it to him... again.

He was convinced Imogen would've happily spent the entire day perusing the collection, but George's eventual protests warned them he'd had enough of being cooped up in his stroller.

She turned with a smile. 'Lunch?'

'I know the perfect place.'

Her lips twitched. 'I just bet you do.'

He took her to Ibirapuera Park. At 158 hectares, it was one of the largest urban parks in Latin America. They bought *pastel de queijos*—delicious deep-fried snacks stuffed with savoury fillings—and meat patties formed around wooden skewers called *kibe*, and sat on the grass to eat them. They spread out a small blanket for George, and he belly-crawled between the two of them, munching on a rusk and cooing his delight at being freed from his pram.

Buskers started up nearby and Imogen leaned towards them as she listened. 'My father would love this so hard.'

Her sound-recording father? He straightened from where he'd been leaning back on his elbows. He'd been trying to think of a way to keep her occupied for the afternoon, and he might've just found it. 'Would you keep an eye on George for ten minutes while I slip off?'

'Sure.'

It took him fifteen minutes, but it was worth it when he lowered his bag of purchases to her lap. She pulled out the mini cassette recorder and the stack of tiny tapes he'd bought, and she turned to him with a question in her eyes. 'I thought you might like to record these guys for your dad…and maybe send your parents a kind of São Paulo diary. I mean, I know you can do that stuff on your phone, but reception is pretty dodgy at Tesoura, and if you wanted to continue the diary there… Anyway, I thought your father might enjoy the older technology.'

'Oh, Jasper, that's a brilliant idea!' She leaned across to George, who sat between them, and tickled his tummy. 'Your uncle has the best ideas, George.' She glanced up, her eyes shining. 'Thank you, it was the perfect thing to do.'

He didn't know how she did it, but she made him feel like a superhero.

She slipped a tape into the recorder and immediately gave the date and location, introducing both George and Jasper and making them say hello into the machine. George's hello was inaudible as he tried to eat the recorder. She rescued it with a laugh and then rested back on one hand and gave her impressions of the city. She recorded the nearby buskers—but not until she'd bought their CD and asked their permission. When they found out she was from Australia they played a Brazilian version of 'Waltzing Matilda' that absolutely delighted her.

Her fun and excitement infected both him and George. Though eventually George snuggled down on his blanket with his bottle, his eyes growing heavy as the afternoon began to lengthen. Imogen collapsed to her knees beside Jasper, gesturing to the buskers. 'They're amazing. My father will love them. This day has been amazing, Jasper. It shouldn't have been but… *you're* amazing.'

And then she leaned forward and pressed her lips to his in a brief, exuberant kiss that had every pulse in his body thumping.

She eased away, still smiling, but it faded as she stared into his eyes. Her lips parted and a yearning he couldn't refuse stretched across her face. In that moment he was lost. Curving a hand around her nape, he drew her head back down to his again and he kissed her with a hunger he didn't bother trying to conceal. Somehow, she ended up in his lap, curled there as if she belonged, her fingers threading through his short hair, her tongue tangling with his and driving him mad with need.

He only came to when a group of passing youths catcalled. *Damn.* What on earth was he thinking? They were supposed to be looking after a baby, not necking like a couple of teenagers!

He set her away from him with more speed

than grace. 'I'm sorry. I promised that wouldn't happen again.'

She paled at whatever she saw in his face. He pulled in a deep breath, tried to moderate his voice. 'Are you okay?'

'I'm fine.' She lifted her chin. '*I'm* not the one who's sorry that happened.' The green in her eyes flashed. 'I *like* kissing you, Jasper. I… I like you.'

He saw then how invested she was becoming—in him…in them. But there was no them. And if he let her continue thinking that, he'd hurt her. Badly. With a force of will, he hardened his heart. 'I like kissing you too, but it won't happen again. Emotions are running high today.'

Her gaze narrowed. 'It's more than that and you know it.'

'And I don't need the complication in my life,' he continued as if she hadn't interrupted. He hated the swift shaft of pain that darkened her eyes. 'Your aunt would never forgive me if I scratched that particular itch with you, especially if I let you think it meant more than it did.'

He waited for her to call him a jackass, but she didn't. She merely turned her back on him and her attention back to the park.

Damn! His life was on a Brazilian island. Hers

was in Australia. Their lives were going in totally opposite directions. Perhaps that in and of itself wasn't such an insurmountable obstacle if it weren't for other things. But there *were* other things—his father, his own reluctance to trust again, his lack of faith and hope. Just...*no*! He wasn't prepared to go through any of that again.

He couldn't give her the kind of long-term relationship she wanted and deserved, so he had no business kissing her. What she deserved was a wholesome, undamaged man who wasn't carrying a ton of baggage and didn't have a family like his waiting to close its jaws about her. She deserved a man who could commit to forever. A man who could protect her rather than one who would bring trouble to her door.

And that man wasn't him.

CHAPTER NINE

IMOGEN STARED AT the doctor the following morning. 'The lump is benign?' she repeated.

'We're ninety per cent certain it's benign,' the doctor clarified. 'We only have the preliminary results—it'll be another five days before the full report is available—but the signs are good.' The doctor smiled. 'But, *sim*, I am confident all is well.'

Jasper leaned towards the statuesque white-coated woman. 'So you don't think Katherine has cancer?'

'That is correct.'

With a whoop, Imogen hugged her aunt, though she was careful not to hug her too tight in case Katherine was still sore from her biopsy. 'Best news ever!'

She turned back to find that Jasper had seized George from his stroller and was holding him aloft like some kind of victory trophy. George loved every moment of it, squealing and kicking his legs.

Katherine seized the doctor's hand and pumped it up and down. 'Thank you so much, Doctor. I can't thank you enough.'

'It will be thanks enough, *minha amiga*, if you keep up to date with your mammograms and promise to make an appointment with your doctor if anything ever again gives you cause for concern.'

'I've learned my lesson. So… I can go now?'

The doctor consulted Katherine's chart. 'I'm afraid not. Mr Coleman has booked you in for a complete medical check. But you should be done by four o'clock this afternoon.'

Katherine turned to Jasper as soon as the doctor left and raised an eyebrow. Imogen did her best not to think about how she and Jasper would survive another day in each other's company.

Not after he'd kissed her. And then acted like a jerk. When prior to that he'd been…

She swallowed. When he'd been every dream she hadn't known she'd wanted. He'd been kind and fun, warm and witty, he'd made her laugh when she hadn't thought that possible. He'd given both her mind and her hands something to do, and while that hadn't rid her of worry for Katherine, it had made it bearable.

Until he'd kissed her, that was. She'd forgotten

everything then—Katherine, George, herself. The kiss had been perfect.

Until it wasn't.

'Imogen, help me out here.'

She snapped back to find an exasperated Katherine staring at her. She'd missed the beginning of the conversation, but she could guess it. 'What's the harm in getting the tests done, Auntie Kay? Mum's wishing she'd gone for an eye test earlier.' She glanced at her watch. 'It's only another six or so hours. I'm happy to hang here and keep you company.'

She didn't want to spend another moment with Jasper, thank you very much. Their stilted conversation and taut silences were wearing on her nerves. After yesterday's kiss he'd retreated with so much unholy speed it'd left her feeling tainted and ugly. And stupid.

It shouldn't matter so much. It shouldn't *hurt* so much. But it did.

Katherine blew out an exasperated breath. 'Fine, I'll have the tests, but I don't want either one of you hanging around the hospital. Go out and see the sights. Have fun.'

Ha! Fun and Jasper no longer went together in the same sentence.

Jasper cleared his throat. 'I actually have some work I need to do.'

He didn't look at her as he spoke.

'Work when you get home,' Katherine protested. 'You and Imogen should go enjoy yourselves.'

'That's okay, Jasper doesn't need to act as my tour guide,' Imogen inserted in her most cheerful voice—so bright it bounced off the walls like a shiny new ten-cent piece. 'What I'd really like to do today is hit the shops. I want to buy souvenirs for everyone back home. I was reading about a market that's under one of the art galleries and it sounds fab—I'm hoping to pick up some pretty, locally made jewellery, maybe find a fabric store or two. I doubt it'd be Jasper's thing.'

'I'd be happy to accompany you.'

But he said it with such a lack of enthusiasm it made even Katherine roll her eyes. Imogen did her best to stop her insides from shrivelling. 'Not necessary. And I'm happy to take George so you can concentrate on your work.' George would be a welcome distraction.

'I can manage.' He set George back in his stroller.

She folded her arms. 'You know he hates being cooped up inside all day.'

His eyes flashed. 'So I'll take him to the park.'

Ha! So he wasn't as cool and reserved as he'd like her to think.

Katherine glanced from one to the other, and Imogen immediately curbed her impulse to get another rise out of him. It was childish. And it'd only make her feel better in the short-term. It'd be best to do what he was doing—put him out of her mind completely. 'Are you sure you wouldn't prefer a bit of company, Auntie Kay?'

'Absolutely not.'

'Then is there anything you'd like me to get for you while I'm out?'

Her aunt made a list, and Imogen didn't know why Jasper hung around if they were going their separate ways for the day. 'You didn't have to wait,' she said as they walked to the elevator.

'I wanted a word with you before you took off.'

But when several people joined them in the elevator he didn't speak again until they stood alone in the wide hospital foyer. The waiting made things inside her clench up. 'It's great news about Katherine's results,' she finally prompted when he'd remained silent for too long.

He turned to her as if he'd forgotten she was

there. Which was great for a girl's ego. She pressed her lips together hard and didn't say a word.

'Look, Imogen, about what happened in the park yesterday—'

'Are you just going to apologise again?' she cut in. 'And remind me you're not interested in a relationship again, blahdy-blah?'

His eyebrows rose. 'Blahdy-blah?'

She lifted an eyebrow of her own, and eventually he nodded. 'Pretty much.'

She gave an exaggerated roll of her eyes designed to annoy him. 'Then *puhlease* spare me and take it as read, okay?' She had the satisfaction of seeing his jaw clench, but it didn't help, not in the slightest. Just as she'd known it wouldn't. 'Was there anything else?'

'Yes,' he snapped, drawing himself up to his full height and becoming a stranger—an autocrat—and it reminded her fiercely that he was her billionaire boss and she was nothing but his lowly maid. 'Can you cook?'

That made her blink. 'I'm no chef, but I can cook a meal without burning it.'

'I want to give Katherine a week's holiday. I'd like to reassign your duties to meal preparation. You've taught me enough now about how to look after a baby that I'm confident I can take care of George without assistance. Needless to say, I'm grateful for all the help you've given me where he's concerned.'

But her help was no longer required. She heard that message loud and clear. This was Jasper Coleman reasserting his authority. She wanted to tell him he was being a pompous jackass. But he wasn't. He was drawing strict and rigid boundaries between them, leaving her in no doubt that he'd meant all he'd said about relationships and complications.

And the sooner her heart got that message, the better. She folded her face into polite lines. 'That won't be a problem. I'd be delighted to assist, sir.'

He blanched at her *sir*. She refused to let herself feel anything. She simply waited for him to either give her further instructions or to dismiss her. Actually, this subservience thing wasn't too hard once she put her mind to it.

'Have a pleasant day, Imogen.'

'Thank you, sir.' She bent down to tickle George's tummy and then turned and walked away before she cried.

After her third day of being Tesoura's head chef, Imogen told herself that she'd finally found her equilibrium. She and Jasper hadn't been able to maintain such an intense formality with each other, not with Katherine playing spectator. But as they hardly spent any time in each other's company, maintaining a polite facade proved no great hardship.

As long as she didn't look at him. As long as she didn't remember the way he'd kissed her in the park. As long as she recited, *You're just the maid* over and over in her mind.

What was proving harder to ignore at the moment was a baby's insistent crying. She turned her clock to face her—2:38 a.m. It appeared Mr I'm-Confident-I-Can-Look-After-George-on-My-Own-Without-Assistance wasn't doing so well in the parenting stakes at the moment.

She was tempted to roll over and pull a pillow over her head, and if it was only Jasper who'd suffer she would. But George…

With a sigh, she hauled herself out of bed, mentally checked what she was wearing—a baggy T-shirt and a pair of tracksuit bottoms, which were far from glamorous but at least covered her decently enough—before heading in the direction of George's wails.

She found Jasper pacing the living room with

a distressed George, who was refusing to take his bottle.

Jasper's eyes flooded with relief when he saw her, but he said, 'I'm sorry I disturbed you. I needed to heat up a bottle and he cries even harder when I put him down.'

She ignored Jasper—it seemed wise—to focus all her attention on the baby. 'Hey, little man. What's the problem?'

He lifted his head to stare at her and held out his arms, his cries easing. She took him and cuddled him close. 'Aw, poor baby. You're hot.'

He opened his mouth and made angry noises and she cooed back soothing sounds as she ran her hand over his damp hair. 'I know, you're trying to tell me what's wrong, aren't you?'

His crying subsided into hiccups and she took the opportunity to run a finger along his gums. Poor little guy had a tooth coming through. Without glancing at Jasper—it was better not to look at him or to think about him, especially not at this time of night—she started for the nursery.

'What are you looking for?' Jasper said when she tried to search one of the bags one-handed.

'His thermometer.'

He took the bag, found the thermometer and

handed it to her. She took George's temperature, crooning to him the entire time.

'Do I need to call a doctor?'

She shook her head, finally risking a glance his way. He looked deliciously dishevelled and heartbreakingly worried. 'His temperature is only up a tiny bit. How long has he been like this?'

'Nearly two and a half hours.'

No wonder he looked so frazzled. 'Why didn't you come and get me?'

'Because I didn't want to come across all feeble and pathetic. But you were my next port of call. How did you get him to stop crying?'

She grimaced. 'I'm going to try and break this as gently as I can—this is a temporary respite. George is teething.'

The nursery was too small, too intimate, too much. She moved towards the door, nodding at the bag Jasper had discarded. 'Let's go back downstairs, but bring that with you.'

She put teething gel on George's gums. But it evidently brought him little relief, as he soon started crying again.

She watched Jasper pace the floor in growing agitation, biting the inside of her lip. 'Would it help if I told you this was entirely normal?'

'A little.' But his eyes said otherwise.

Whatever else had happened between them, she couldn't deny that he loved his nephew. She flashed to the day of Katherine's scheduled biopsy—the way he'd taken her to the exhibition and had then urged her to record a message and playlist for her parents, the way he'd helped draw her mind from her worry. She needed to find a way to distract him like that.

'Can you access Jupiter's social media account from your phone?'

'Yes.'

'I think we should post something to her timeline now.'

He pulled out his phone. 'What do you want it to say?'

'Pacing the floor with a teething nine-month-old. Have tried a bottle, teething ring and teething gel so far, and lots of walking and rocking. So far nothing has helped. Any tips?'

He glanced up and she couldn't read the expression in his eyes. 'If you say one thing about bed hair,' she warned.

'There's absolutely nothing wrong with your hair, Imogen. You're hoping Emily reads this, aren't you?'

She shrugged.

'You're a genius.'

'*Not* a genius. Just not afraid to ask for help. There's a wealth of experience out there on social media. Why not tap into it?' If, at the same time, they could pique a mother's maternal concern...

His phone pinged.

'Guardian Angel 27 says "Pray".'

'Helpful.'

More pings sounded. 'Janice sends "lots of hugs".'

It was nice of her, but not exactly helpful either.

'"Iced water",' he read out.

Her lips twitched. 'That's a little ambiguous. Are we supposed to give it to him to drink or douse ourselves in it?'

His gaze didn't leave his phone. 'Um... "Hang him upside down whilst you drink a margarita."'

'Just...no.'

He scanned through the replies that were evidently pouring in, and then stilled. 'You won't believe this, but Emily has just responded.'

She leaned towards him. 'What does she say?'

'That last time her bub was teething, putting him in his stroller with his comfort toy and pushing the stroller back and forth helped.'

'I'm putting him in his stroller.' She started for the front foyer, which was where the stroller was currently parked.

'I'll grab his bunny.'

Jasper's heart pounded as the baby's cries started to abate.

Imogen nudged his foot and he realised she'd been talking to him and he hadn't been paying attention—hadn't heard a word.

'Tell her George's crying is easing and that it looks like it's working.'

He started typing on his phone.

'Georgia!' she corrected. 'Say Georgia.'

He backspaced, heart and head both racing. He nearly handed her the phone, his fingers feeling like thumbs, but…

But he was finally talking to Emily. His sister. After two years she'd finally spoken to him again, and he hadn't realised it would mean so much.

A personal message hit his inbox, and he immediately opened it. Need help.

He wanted to ring, but if Aaron was nearby… 'What can I do?' he typed back.

His phone rang. 'Emily?'

'Jasper.'

He didn't bother with preliminaries or pleasantries. 'What do you need?'

'I need to get away from Aaron. If he gets hold of me now, he'll kill me.'

He doubted she was exaggerating. 'I can get you on a plane first thing in the morning, for either Rio or São Paulo. Hold on...' He strode into his office, aware of a silent Imogen coming to stand in the doorway with the stroller to watch and listen as he made the travel arrangements on his computer. 'Have you got pen and paper there, Em?'

He gave her the flight details. He organised a bodyguard to accompany her from Sydney to Rio. He organised a private charter from Rio to Tesoura.

'Are you safe from Aaron tonight?'

'I'm at a safe house. He's away on business but will be back tomorrow. Look, Jasper, he's involved in some kind of money-laundering racket, and I've been helping the police with their enquiries. It's about to come to a head soon...'

'Does he know that?'

'I don't know, but I don't want to be anywhere near him when he does.'

'I won't let that happen. Give me the address

of where you're staying. I'm sending that body-guard tonight.'

'I'm going to have to ditch my phone. He'll be able to track me on it.'

'I'll have a new one couriered to you.' She needed to be able to contact him in case any-thing happened.

'How's…how's George?'

'He's the sweetest, happiest little guy, Em. I don't know how you've managed it.'

'I've missed him so much, but Aaron has been so…unpredictable lately.'

Jasper closed his eyes.

'I needed to send George somewhere safe—away from everything that's happening here—in case things blew up earlier than expected.'

'Where does Aaron think he is?'

'With Auntie Pat. I told him I wanted to go and stay with her for a few days while he was away on business.'

He'd bet Aaron hadn't liked that. Pat was their mother's sister, and she loathed Keith. Which meant she probably loathed Aaron too.

'Tomorrow you and George will be reunited and safe, I promise.'

'I can't thank you enough, Jasper.'

'No need.'

They rang off. He turned to meet Imogen's gaze. She looked as if she meant to take a step towards him but pulled back at the last moment. 'Emily is coming?'

He nodded.

'That's…that's amazing news.'

She glanced down at the stroller, stopped pushing and lifted crossed fingers. Not a peep came from George. He'd finally fallen asleep.

With a brisk movement, she turned and headed upstairs. Jasper eased past the pram and followed her. 'What are you…?'

He trailed off when she checked the two currently vacant guest rooms. 'We'll give her this one.'

It was the room next to George's and had its own en suite bathroom. She grabbed a fresh set of sheets from the linen cupboard and started to make up the bed. He immediately kicked forward to help. 'There'll be time to do this tomorrow, you know?'

'I know, but I'm awake now.'

She shot him a grin and it made things inside him burn. He'd missed that smile. And her sense of fun. He shook himself. It didn't matter how much his heart protested. The distance he'd deliberately put between them was still for the best.

'I warn you now, though, breakfast is going to be a lacklustre affair.'

'Forget breakfast. I'll get some cereal and toast when I'm ready. Sleep as late as you like. I plan to.'

'Liar. You probably won't sleep a wink until Emily is here.'

She was probably right.

He followed her gaze as it ran about the room. 'What?'

'This is a nice room, but I'm wondering how we can make it more homey. I'll put a vase of flowers on the dresser.' She glanced in at the en suite bathroom. 'I bought some pretty toiletries while I was on the mainland. They'll do nicely in here.'

His chest hitched. 'You don't have to give your things away, Imogen.'

'I don't mind. Besides, I think your sister deserves a little pampering. And I know you'll want her to feel…'

'Safe? Unafraid?'

She nodded. 'But also at home. As if nothing

bad could possibly happen to her here. That it's okay for her to let down her guard and rest.'

She put it into words better than he ever could have.

She glanced at him then with unabashed admiration. 'You thought of everything—on the fly—without a moment of panic, when she rang and asked for help. You were confident and in command of the situation—which must've been so reassuring for her. It was amazing to witness. She's lucky to have you, Jasper.'

An itch started up between his shoulder blades. Nothing could happen between him and this woman—he would not let his family destroy her the way it had him and Emily. But he owed her. And he could give her something now—a part of himself he'd never given to anyone. 'Immy, I've played that scenario—Emily ringing me like that—in my mind hundreds, maybe a thousand, times.'

Shortening her name seemed natural and right, so he didn't bother questioning it. 'Ever since I arrived on Tesoura I've wanted Emily to call and ask me to help her break free from Aaron.' He gave a low laugh. 'Which probably means I have some kind of saviour complex.'

'Nonsense.' She moved a step closer, her hands

pressed to her chest. 'It means you love your sister and you want her to be safe and happy.'

He tried to not look at her chest, at the way her hands—pressed against thin cotton—highlighted curves that made him ache. He forced his gaze back to hers. 'On the outside I might've appeared calm during that phone call, but on the inside, I was anything but.'

Her eyes softened and her lips parted. Wind roared in his ears and fire licked along his veins. He eased back a step, feeling anything but calm now. She glanced at him and then at the freshly made bed and colour mounted high on her cheeks. Everything inside him clenched. *No!* He would not take advantage of this lovely woman. 'I've been meaning to ask, when are you returning to Australia?'

She stared as if she hadn't heard him, and then her head rocked back. 'I… I hadn't set a firm date.' She swallowed. 'You evidently think I should.'

He forced himself to nod. 'You have the launch of your sewing business to prepare for, and…' His mind went blank as he fought the urge to take his words back and beg her to stay.

Her chin lifted but the sparkle in her eyes had dulled. 'I'll talk it over with my aunt and let you know.' She edged towards the door. 'I'm going back to bed. George?'

'I'll take care of him.'

She left, but it was a long time before he could move, before he could rid himself of the foul taste that coated his tongue.

The reunion between Emily and George was a revelation. The way George's face lit up…the love in Emily's face… It made Jasper's throat thicken and he had to clear it a couple of times. Imogen, who hovered nearby ready to leap in and help with anything if it was needed, swiped at her eyes.

She went to disappear back into the kitchen, but he caught hold of her hand. 'Emily, this is Imogen. And heaven help us all if she hadn't been here to help with George—teaching me all I needed to know about babies.' And about being an uncle, he realised now. She'd helped to thaw some of the frozen parts inside him. So had George.

'He's been a perfect doll,' Imogen assured Emily now. 'Haven't you, little man?' she said, tickling his tummy and making him gurgle out a delighted laugh.

Jasper froze. The tableau that the two women

and the baby made…the fact his sister was *in his house…*

He recalled a time when he'd once gone skiing. He'd become so cold that when he'd walked back inside the warm lodge, his face and extremities had burned and ached for a full ten minutes before they'd started to feel normal again. That was how he felt on the inside now.

'I know how long that flight is from Sydney,' Imogen said. 'I'm thinking you'd probably love a chance to freshen up. Why don't I show you to your room?'

He trailed along behind them. So many emotions pounded through him in such quick succession it left him feeling disembodied. Happiness, grief, anger, protectiveness, relief—they all wrestled inside him.

'It's a beautiful room.' Emily's gaze zeroed in on the photo of George sitting on the bedside table. Imogen had taken it on her phone and had sent it to Jasper to print out before she'd placed it there in a pretty frame. 'Oh, Jasper, thank you so much!'

She threw an arm about his neck—her other held George clasped to her hip. George cuddled Jasper's arm and something that had been broken inside him started to knit back together.

When Emily released him, Imogen moved across to the bedside table and opened the top drawer. 'I took the liberty of grabbing you a few personal items.'

Emily moved across to glance inside. She stilled before meeting Imogen's gaze. 'Thank you.'

Curiosity shifted through him and he started to move across, and then stopped. They were probably referring to feminine hygiene products. Not that he was the least squeamish or embarrassed about such things, but a woman was entitled to her privacy.

'Is there anything else you need? Anything else I can do?' Imogen asked.

Emily shook her head. 'You've been so kind, thank you.' She glanced at them both, hesitating. 'I'd just love an hour to rest and…and to spend some time alone with George.'

She looked scared—as if she was afraid he would refuse her that…as if she'd started to equate all men's attitudes and behaviours with Aaron's and their father's. It pierced him to the core. 'Take as long as you want. Let me—' it occurred to him then that she might be more comfortable around another woman '—or Imogen know if there's anything you need or anything we can do.'

She nodded, and he left the room, stumbled down the hall to his own bedroom. Slumping down to the bed, he dropped his head to his hands and tried to stem the tears that scalded his eyes.

There was a soft sound in the doorway, and then a pair of arms went around him and pressed his head gently to the softness of her stomach. Imogen. He didn't need to open his eyes to know her. He knew her by her scent, by the sound of her movements, and by the way his every atom came to life at her nearness. He wrapped his arms about her middle and held her tight until the burning stopped. Only then did he ease away.

'Sorry.' His voice came out gruff. He felt vulnerable, exposed…embarrassed. 'What a big baby. I—'

She cupped his face and lifted it to meet her gaze. 'This is a normal human response to an overload of emotion. You've been on this island on your own for far too long, have kept too much bottled up.' She bit her lip, her eyes troubled. 'And despite her make-up, I know you saw her bruises too.'

He had. They were old bruises and were fading, but it hadn't stopped him from wanting to punch something—preferably Aaron. 'She's so thin.'

She swiped the pads of her thumbs beneath his eyes. 'That, at least, is something we can fix, right?'

He nodded. She dropped her hands and eased away. 'It's time for me to get back down to the kitchen.'

With a smile, she was gone.

Over the course of the following week, Emily did put on weight—her cheeks filled out and her eyes started to lose their shadows. Katherine received her full test results, which verified the findings of the preliminary report—she didn't have breast cancer. It gave her the impetus to finish her book and send it off to her editor, and to resume her housekeeping duties. Meanwhile, Jasper desperately tried to think of a way to tempt Imogen back into the water for her daily swims.

She hadn't been for a single dip since they'd returned from São Paulo. He had an uncomfortable feeling he was to blame, but he didn't know how or why, and he desperately wanted to make amends. She'd arranged her return flights to Australia and now only had another week before she left. That was all—*one single week*! He wanted to make it as pleasant for her as he could.

And he definitely didn't want to think about how he'd feel once she was gone.

'What's on your mind?' Emily said from her spot on the floor where she played with George.

'Imogen.'

'Hmm…'

He glanced up at the knowing note in his sister's voice when the front door crashed open with a bang that made them all jump. Aaron appeared in the doorway. His shadow seemed to darken the room. Emily gave a strangled cry, her hand flying to her mouth. Jasper shot to his feet. Little George pulled himself up on unsteady legs and hurled himself at Jasper, clinging to his leg and hiding his face against it.

'I knew this was where you'd be, you traitorous cow!'

Jasper fought the urge to move across and punch the other man. Emily and George had seen enough violence, had been through enough.

At that moment Imogen came walking down the stairs with an armful of dirty linen. 'Do we have another visitor?' she called out cheerfully. 'Should I make up another room?'

'No need,' Aaron said with a snarl as she reached the bottom of the stairs. 'My wife, son and I won't be staying.'

'I see.' She pursed her lips, staring up at him. She looked tiny beside him. 'I take it you're Aaron?'

He gave a thin-lipped smile that made Jasper's heart pound so hard it almost hurt. He handed Jasper to Emily and started across the room, but before he could reach them, Imogen calmly lifted an arm and sprayed Aaron full in the face with something that had the other man immediately screaming and dropping to his knees. 'Agh, help! She's thrown acid in my face!'

She stepped over him and handed the can of spray to Emily. 'I knew that was going to be a good investment. Pepper spray,' she added for Jasper's benefit. 'I know it's not legal in New South Wales, but when I saw a can of it in São Paulo I figured it wouldn't hurt to have some.'

He didn't know what to say. He couldn't believe how...how *efficiently* she'd handled a potentially deadly situation.

Katherine came through from the kitchen. 'I've called the police. They're on their way.' She tossed Jasper a roll of duct tape. 'Tie him up for his own safety. Before Imogen is tempted to hurt him some more. And, Jasper,' she added, 'I wouldn't be too gentle about it if I were you.'

As much as he wanted to, he couldn't hit a defenceless man, and at the moment Aaron was nothing but a helpless, snivelling mess.

The police arrived an hour later and took him away. Emily and George retired to her room for a rest. Katherine returned to the kitchen. Jasper stared at Imogen. 'You really are something.'

She shrugged, but it didn't hide the way her hands had started to shake. 'I was pretty amazing, huh?'

He pulled her into his arms, pressing his lips to her hair. 'You scared me half out of my wits.'

CHAPTER TEN

KEITH COLEMAN ARRIVED two days later.

'Jasper,' Katherine called out from the living room. 'Your father is on the supply boat. It'll have docked by now, so he'll be here any minute.'

Jasper came out from his office where he'd been digitising Imogen's tapes for her. He couldn't decide if he was surprised by this turn of events or not. He glanced across at Emily, who'd paled, but she kept a resolute angle to her chin. Beside her, George crab-walked the length of the sofa, holding on to it for balance. The kid was going to be a runner when he grew up—a top-class athlete.

When he glanced back up, Imogen had appeared at her aunt's shoulder. Everything inside him clamoured at the mere sight of her. Ever since he'd watched her approach Aaron, fear had filled his soul. He'd wake in the middle of the night in a cold sweat from dreams where she was in trouble and he couldn't get to her in time.

Not that she'd needed him to come to her rescue two days ago. She'd rescued all of them instead.

The fact was she didn't need *him*.

The front door rattled and then shouting and pounding followed when it didn't open.

George fell to his nappy-clad bottom. Emily picked him up and cuddled him. Katherine's brows rose. 'The door's locked?'

'Oh, didn't I mention it? I've taken to locking it.' Imogen shrugged with an utter lack of concern.

Jasper wanted to smile at her complete disregard for his father's impatience—growing louder by the second. And then he wanted to hit something. Was she afraid to stay here since Aaron's unexpected arrival? Was—?

'Should I get it?' She pointed to the door.

He blew out a breath and nodded. 'Chin up, Em. I won't let him hurt you.'

'I know. It's like this is the final hurdle, and then I'll be free.'

He kept his gaze trained on Imogen as she moved towards the door. She opened it with a scolding, 'Heavens, what a racket. Really, sir, the doorbell is in perfect working order. Now, how can I help you?'

'I'm Mr Keith Coleman, and I demand to see my daughter and son. I *will* see them and no damn servant is going to stop me.'

Jasper moved into view before Keith could push Imogen out of the way. If his father touched her, he knew he wouldn't be able to think straight. And it'd be better for all concerned that he kept this as civilised as possible. From behind Imogen, he met Keith's glare. 'If you so much as lay one finger on any person here on my island, I will beat you to a bloody pulp and then take you a mile out that way—' he pointed seawards '—and drop your sorry butt overboard.' He kept his voice pleasant for George's and Emily's sakes.

Keith's mouth worked, but no sound came out.

Imogen glanced at Jasper and he nodded. She opened the door wider. 'Why don't you step inside, Mr Coleman?'

Keith straightened his suit jacket before stalking into the living room.

Emily stood and Jasper went to stand beside her. Imogen moved back beside her aunt. Keith sneered at them all. 'You think you have the upper hand, but you're wrong.'

Once upon a time a veiled threat like that

would've had Jasper turning cold with dread. Now he saw through the bluster to the ugly bully beneath.

Keith stabbed a finger at Emily. 'I demand you return to your husband immediately.'

'You want her to return to a dangerous criminal?' Jasper kinked an eyebrow. 'How very egalitarian of you.' He couldn't believe his father hadn't washed his hands of his son-in-law and put as much distance between himself and Aaron as he could, given Aaron's allegedly illegal activities.

The older man dismissed that with a wave of his hand. 'It's all a misunderstanding. And one that will be more quickly cleared up with Emily at home by her husband's side.'

'That's not going to happen.' Emily lifted her chin. 'I won't be returning to Aaron. Ever. I'm filing for divorce, and I hope he rots in prison.'

Keith's eyes narrowed to slits. 'If you don't do as I say I'll have you declared an unfit mother. I'll sue for custody of George.'

'You can try, but you won't succeed. I've been planning my escape for months. I know my rights. I've photographic evidence of the bruises Aaron's given me. And I think it's safe to assume that Jasper will provide me with the very best family lawyers available.'

'Goes without saying,' Jasper murmured, proud of the way she held her ground.

'And if you do take this to court, Father, I'll tell the police that you and Aaron wanted me to perjure myself in court and say that Jasper's attack on Aaron two years ago was unprovoked.'

'Why, you little—' He broke off, his eyes narrowing. 'Your mother will pay for your disobedience.' He clenched a hand, that fist leaving none of them in doubt as to how he meant to make her pay. From the corner of his eye, Jasper saw Imogen flinch and had to bottle down his instant desire to plant a fist in his father's face.

He wasn't his father.

'Mother doesn't deserve the way you treat her, but I can't take responsibility for that any more.'

Emily's words made Jasper blink. Had she stayed with Aaron all this time to protect and support their mother?

Giving a derisory snort, the older man turned his attention to Katherine. 'I know what you've been up to. I've been keeping tabs.'

Katherine's eyes went mock wide. 'How thrilling for you, Keith.'

'I could make you a laughing stock—expose

the ludicrous stuff you write to everyone you know.'

Jasper's gut clenched, but Imogen gave a barely stifled giggle. 'He has no idea about the world of genre fiction, does he, Auntie Kay?'

'None.'

Imogen winked at Jasper, who must've also looked at a loss because she added, 'Katherine's more likely to be swamped by adoring fans than mocked. I mean, there's bound to be the odd literary snob, but—'

'But not anyone we need concern ourselves with,' Katherine said.

'I know who your agent is. I know the name of your editor. Your publisher is a member of my club.'

Ice tripped down Jasper's spine. Keith would ruin Kate's career? The sense of déjà vu, of helplessness, rose up through him.

Katherine folded her arms. 'The thing is, publishing houses can be sold. I'm quite certain that Jasper could be prevailed upon to buy a publishing house, and to maybe even make me one of his lead authors.'

His panic dissipated, his heartbeat steadied. 'I've always fancied becoming a patron of the arts.'

The smile Imogen sent him was worth the price of two publishing houses.

'I know all about *you* too, Imogen Hartley. And you needn't think you're out of my reach.'

Jasper's every sense went on high alert.

'If you and your aunt don't want any trouble, you'll both leave this island now…*today*.'

'Or?' she inquired with a polite lift of her brows.

'Or you'll find the lease for your business premises has disappeared and the space mysteriously let to someone else. Or maybe the zoning laws will have changed…and then your planning-permission paperwork might go astray.'

She glanced at Jasper. 'He really is an unpleasant piece of work. You and Emily have my sympathies.'

Acid burned his chest. She was leaving in five days anyway. Her leaving today would make no difference. This wasn't her fight. She had a life to get back to. He steeled himself for her nod of acceptance and tried to control the nausea swirling through him.

She folded her arms. 'You're a slimy eel of a man, Mr Coleman.'

Jasper stiffened. What was she doing? Couldn't she see the danger of kicking the hornets' nest?

'You don't see it, do you?' she continued. 'The tables are turning…the power is shifting. Jasper would buy me the perfect premises and hire a business lawyer on my behalf—just to make sure all my paperwork was in order—if I asked it of him. And I'd rather take my chances with him than with you, thank you very much.'

He stilled. It hit him then—Imogen would always choose to do what was right rather than what was easy. She wasn't like Bronwyn. She was a woman who would stay and fight for him. For a moment he could barely breathe.

And then his heart swelled.

'But he won't be able to prevent the bad publicity of a smear campaign. I'll make sure word gets around that your workmanship is substandard and your ethics questionable.'

The threat rocked her, Jasper could see that, but her chin didn't drop. 'Like I said, I'll take my chances.'

'You're fools, the lot of you. You—' he swung back to Jasper '—will return to Australia at my side tomorrow and help me fix this sorry mess or I'll destroy them all.'

Jasper's mind raced. Imogen's words going round and round in his mind—*the power is shifting*. Why hadn't Keith disassociated himself from Aaron? Why hadn't he claimed ignorance of the man's activities and thrown him to the wolves? Keith had done that more than once in his political career to so-called trusted colleagues. Unless…

Jasper widened his stance. Unless he was involved in Aaron's illegal activities too.

All the pieces of the puzzle fell into place. The reason Keith had championed Emily and Aaron's relationship. The reason he'd renounced Jasper before his son could work out what was going on. His desperation now.

Jasper no longer feared his father. He might not be able to nullify all the harm Keith could do, but the women in this room had just shown him how he could mitigate it.

He didn't want to mitigate it, though. He wanted to *demolish* it. He recalled his father's threats to Imogen, and his resolve hardened to tempered steel. He wasn't letting the man get away with that. He was *not* going to let him hurt Imogen. Not now. Not ever.

His every thought sharpened—honed by years of imagining all the ways he could bring Keith to justice. An image fixed itself in his mind. He'd been digitising Imogen's tapes. That recording equipment was sitting in the top drawer of his desk.

Keith obviously interpreted Jasper's silence for apprehension because he gave a triumphant laugh that made Jasper's skin crawl. 'You always were a soft touch. It was your downfall. You'll do what's right by these women.'

'Why don't we take this discussion into my office? Katherine, could you organise refreshments, please?'

Katherine didn't so much as blink, but Emily grabbed his arm and stared up into his face with earnest eyes. 'Don't do this, Jasper. *Please.*'

It hurt that she had so little faith in him, but he couldn't blame her—not given her experiences with their father and Aaron.

He ignored Emily's plea to glance across at Imogen. 'Make up a guest room for my father.'

Her brow pleated. 'What are you doing? Why don't you just boot him off the island and—?'

'I'm doing what's necessary.'

'But—'

He moved across to her. 'Don't make things harder than they have to be.' He made sure the words carried across to his father. He made sure his next ones didn't. 'Slap me across the face and flounce off to the kitchen.'

She took a step away from him her eyes going wide, and then her face darkened, and she did as he'd requested—she slapped him.

The imprint of her hand burned against his cheek and he wanted to kiss her. He squashed the impulse as the kitchen door slammed behind her. Emily raced off after her with George in her arms, while he gestured for his father to precede him into his office.

'She's a fiery little piece,' Keith said.

'And fired after that little display,' Jasper returned.

'Pity, you could've had some fun taming her.'

His father's words made his stomach turn, but he didn't betray it by so much as a flicker of an eyelash. He waved to a drinks cabinet on the other side of the room. 'There's a very good aged single malt there. Help yourself.'

While his father's back was turned, he moved behind his desk, opened his top drawer and placed a blank cassette into the mini-recorder before slipping it into the pocket of his jacket. This morning when he'd pulled on a suit jacket, he'd told himself it was an attempt to return to a sense of normalcy—that he was once again ready to take a conference call if the occasion required it. Imogen had taken one look at him and had shaken her head. He was glad now he'd taken the trouble, though. The jacket felt like armour.

His father returned with two glasses of whisky. Jasper took one and sat, gestured for his father to take a seat too. 'You ought to know I'm not the inexperienced boy I once was. The business world has taught me a lot. It's not possible to achieve the amount of success I have while keeping all of one's ideals and scruples…intact.'

He pretended to sip his Scotch as he let his father draw conclusions—undoubtedly unfavourable—about his son's business practices.

Imogen's face rose in his mind, solidifying his intent. 'I'm not easily browbeaten. And I'm not going to pretend I am now.'

'If you don't do as I tell you, those women will suffer. I'll make it a personal crusade. While I'd be a fool to say such things in front of witnesses, accidents can be arranged.'

'Yes, they can.'

He let those words sink in before continuing. 'However, while your threats have little impact on me, I *am* a businessman. I like to make money. And I find myself growing tired of island life.'

Keith's eyes narrowed. 'What are you proposing?'

'I won't make Emily return to Aaron.'

His father started to rise. 'But—'

'The man's a fool for getting caught. I'm sure there's a way to…deal with him.'

Keith subsided, his eyes starting to gleam. 'Deal with him how?'

'I'm sure you can think of something. I'll only agree to return to Australia if you cut me in on whatever scheme you and Aaron have going.'

Keith started to laugh. These were the kinds of deals his father was used to making. 'You think I'd trust you with anything of that kind?'

'Money can buy a lot of things. Including information.'

Keith leaned back as if he held all the cards. 'Are you offering me money?'

'No, I don't owe you a thing. You owe me. And if I return to Australia…' He let the sentence hang for a moment. '*If* I return to Australia it'll be on an equal footing, *not* as your dogsbody.'

Keith's face twisted, and he slammed his glass down. 'You want to cut me out—take control of everything!' Because that was the way his father's mind worked.

Jasper gave a negligent shrug. 'Just like you, I find I have a taste for power. I want to be top dog.' He wanted to make sure Keith could never threaten Imogen again.

Keith thumped his chest. 'I'm top dog. I'm the one who has the contacts and knows how everything fits together. If I cut you in, it'll be on my terms.'

'But that said,' he continued, as if his father hadn't spoken, 'I'm sure my money could be put to use in advantageous and creative ways that would be in everyone's best interests.'

He broke off when a knock sounded. Katherine entered with a tray bearing coffee and warm scones. She set it on the desk. 'Will there be anything else?'

Jasper glanced at his father and let his lips lift as if in expectation that a deal would be struck soon. 'I think we'll have the fillet steak for dinner tonight, Katherine.'

It was his father's favourite, and predictably the older man preened as if he'd somehow won. Stupid man. Keith was going to find out exactly what happened when he threatened the people his son loved.

Katherine closed the door on her way out. Jasper set a mug of coffee in front of Keith. 'I'll need some kind of guarantee before I commit any money to the project.'

Keith seemed to think that over, knocked back the rest of his Scotch before setting it down with a nod. 'I can tell you enough to realise any financial investment you make would be well rewarded.'

Jasper lifted his coffee to his lips. 'I'm listening.'

'Let me get this straight,' Emily repeated. 'Jasper *asked* you to slap him?'

Imogen nodded. 'He's up to something. He has a plan, so don't lose heart. Your father doesn't frighten him.'

Emily let George scramble down from her lap to retrieve his bunny. 'I hope you're right.'

She was right. Jasper had a plan. She just prayed he could pull it off.

'I must say, Immy, you certainly responded to his request with…enthusiasm,' Katherine said.

'I wanted to be convincing.'

Had she channelled all her anger into that slap? Anger that he'd kissed her and then rejected her.

Anger that it continued to mean so much. She swallowed. 'Do you think I hurt him?'

Katherine's eyes danced. 'Let's just say that I think it'll keep him focussed.'

She'd hated hitting him. The moment after she'd struck him, she'd wanted to take that beautiful face in her hands and kiss it better—it was why she'd flounced away in such a rush. Instinct told her that Jasper was playing some deep game, and the stakes were high. She'd help him in whatever way she could—because she trusted him and wanted to support him—and he'd be grateful. But she had to be careful not to read anything more into it than that.

She wasn't giving him any further reason to tell her that while he was attracted to her, he didn't want anything more. He'd been honest with her from the start. Why couldn't she have got that straight in her head? Why did she have to go and fall for him?

'Right, Imogen, you'd better go and get that room ready.'

Emily twisted her hands together. 'I don't want to sleep in the same part of the house as my father.'

Imogen didn't blame her. 'My room has twin

beds if you want to bunk in with me. I mean, it's nothing fancy, but…'

The relief that raced across Emily's face was all the answer she needed. 'C'mon, I'll make up a room for Sir Keith the Jackass and then we can move your things downstairs for the night.' Including that can of pepper spray.

The rest of the afternoon dragged by, the suspense that hung in the air making it hard to concentrate on anything. Emily had her dinner in the kitchen with Imogen and Katherine. Jasper and his father ate in the dining room where Imogen couldn't help noticing how at home Keith made himself.

Ha! What did she mean, *couldn't help noticing*? She was spying. Of course she could help noticing. She was *deliberately* noticing.

And what she deliberately noticed was that Keith did most of the talking—all of it bragging and big-noting himself, name-dropping and blowing his own trumpet in relation to his access to Australia's highest political powers. The slimy toad. Jasper, on the other hand, kept calmly plying the man with a very good burgundy—four bottles of the stuff, to be precise—and very little of it made its way down its owner's throat. She crossed her fingers and hoped that whatever Jasper's goal happened to be, he achieved it.

'Your father can drink a lot,' she said, closing the kitchen door quietly and returning to the table where Katherine had brought out a deck of cards and told them they were playing gin rummy. George had long since been put to bed in his cot in Imogen's room.

'Like a fish,' Emily agreed. 'Jasper's going to need a lot of wine if he's hoping to get him drunk.'

Katherine dealt out the cards. 'Then it's just as well your brother keeps his cellar well stocked.'

They played cards for nearly two hours. The next time she peeked, Imogen watched Jasper half carry his very drunk father upstairs, presumably to bed. When he came back downstairs, he went straight into his study without so much as a glance in the direction of the kitchen.

She shifted her weight from one foot to the other, biting the inside of her cheek. She really wanted to go to him, but on what pretext? If he wanted her, he knew where to find her.

Acid burned her stomach. He didn't want her, though. As much as she might want to, she couldn't lose sight of that fact.

Katherine gave her a nudge. 'Go and find out

if there's anything else he needs, and tell him we're locking ourselves in.'

She turned in surprise.

Katherine held up a key. 'The staff quarters lock.'

'Is that necessary?'

'It'll make Emily feel safer.'

She was halfway to Jasper's office when she realised her aunt hadn't actually answered her question. Which was probably an answer in itself. Stomach churning, she tapped on the open office door. Jasper glanced up from where he furiously typed on his computer. 'There's nothing else I need for the evening, Imogen,' he said, pre-empting her. 'You're free to retire.'

Lucky her.

'Emily is bunking in with me tonight. And George.'

He nodded and returned to his computer. 'Was there anything else?' he finally said, not looking at her.

Her chest tightened. He wasn't going to tell her what he was up to? What his plan was? She frowned at a spot on the carpet. 'Katherine told me to tell you we're locking ourselves in.'

He swivelled to face her. 'That's not necessary. But if it makes you feel better...'

What would make her feel better was if he swept her up in his arms and kissed her, told her he'd die without her. Her lips twisted. But that evidently wasn't going to happen.

His eyes swept across her face, and his jaw clenched. He turned back to his computer. 'Goodnight, Imogen.'

She turned and left without uttering another word.

'What did he say?' Emily said the moment she marched back into the kitchen. 'How did he seem?'

High-handed. Remote. Autocratic. She bit the words back. They weren't fair. 'Preoccupied… and uncommunicative.'

'Never mind.' Katherine marshalled them towards the staff quarters. 'Tomorrow may reveal all.'

Imogen tried to rein in her confusion, her hurt. Jasper didn't owe her anything beyond a fair wage and decent working conditions. Her pique faded, but she refused to let hopelessness take its place. Her future held lots of good things— oodles of them. It just didn't include Jasper.

She lifted her chin. Being here on the island had taught her an important lesson. Sometimes you had to take a risk—and if you worked hard and planned well it paid dividends. Some risks *were* worth taking. Look at Aunt Katherine—she'd dared to dream, and it had led to a publishing deal. Emily had risked her own safety to forge a new life for her and George.

Katherine and Emily had faced their fears and both their lives were the better for it. She could face her fears too. She *wasn't* stupid. She *wasn't* naïve and unprepared. She and her business *would* thrive. As for Jasper…

Instinct told her he was taking a big risk now. With all her heart, she hoped it paid off, hoped he vanquished his demons where his father was concerned. And that he had the chance to lead a good and happy life. Her eyes burned. It was what he deserved.

CHAPTER ELEVEN

EDUARDO APPEARED THE following morning as Imogen served breakfast in the dining room. He hovered by the kitchen door, evidently waiting for her.

The scent of freshly cooked bacon—normally a smell she relished—made her stomach turn. Or maybe that was simply her employer's guest. She finished refilling Jasper's and Keith's coffee mugs before moving across to him. She listened as he gave his message in halting English.

'Is there a problem?' Jasper demanded in some kind of boss voice that set her teeth on edge.

She moved back to the table, hands folded at her waist. 'Eduardo tells me there's a boat here. The skipper claims he's been hired to take someone to the mainland.'

Keith smirked. 'Now you'll get your comeuppance, missy. You might think twice before losing your temper again.'

The passage to the mainland was for her?

But…she had another four days before she had to leave. She wasn't ready to go yet. She—

'Call the others in, Imogen.'

As Eduardo hadn't left the doorway, and Katherine and Emily had come to stand behind him, Imogen didn't need to call anyone over. They all moved to stand beside her.

'I have something here I think you'll all be interested in hearing.'

Jasper pulled her mini-recorder from his pocket and hit play. She listened, at first in confusion, but then in growing comprehension as Keith's voice droned on, bragging about offshore bank accounts, complex financial transactions designed to camouflage where money came from, Ponzi schemes and the killing to be made in digital currencies. On the tape, Jasper asked leading questions about how Keith saw his son fitting into this mini-empire of white-collar crime, and Keith gave detailed explanations. She couldn't believe the man had fallen for it! His enormous ego and inflated sense of his own power—his stubborn belief that he could still cow and manipulate Jasper—was his undoing.

'You recorded me?' Keith leapt to his feet, ejected the tape and ground it beneath his heel on the tiles, before shredding the roll of plastic film that had recorded his damning words. He bared his teeth, his breath noisy in the silence. 'You're going to pay for this.'

Jasper didn't appear the least bit perturbed by Keith's actions so she chose not to be either.

'You were so confident you could get me onside. And so ridiculously sure that you were safe telling me everything because there was no one else to bear witness—your word against mine. And as you'd already discredited my character back in Australia, who'd believe an embittered son over a respected politician, right?'

Keith gave an ugly laugh and held up the shredded tape. 'And without this, it's still your word against mine.'

'The tape you're holding is a copy. After I put you to bed last night, I spent the rest of the evening digitising the contents of the tape and sending the electronic file through to the Australian Federal Police. The original is in my safe.'

Keith's face turned purple and then grey.

'As we speak, your house in Sydney is being searched. I've spoken to Mother and told her what's happening, and she's decided to throw her lot in with me rather than take any more abuse from you.'

'She wouldn't dare! I'll—'

'You'll do nothing, because more likely than not you'll be banged up in a jail cell next door to Aaron. You're in no position to do anything.'

'The ungrateful—'

'When you hit someone enough they'll eventually bite back.'

Imogen watched the scene play out in front of her and wanted to cheer…and throw up…and hug Jasper, Emily and George…and the Australian Federal Police.

'You're now a person of interest and a warrant has been issued for your arrest. Police officers will be here in—' he glanced at his watch '—an hour or two, I suspect. So you can wait for them, or you can take your chances evading them on the mainland and leave on the boat that's just arrived. Up to you.'

The older man slammed to his feet. 'I'll make you pay for this. All of you.'

He raced upstairs—presumably to pack. 'Don't let him out of your sight,' Jasper said to Eduardo.

Less than thirty minutes later, the boat pulled away from the dock with Keith Coleman on board.

'Why did you let him go?' Emily almost wailed as she stared after the departing vessel.

'I didn't let him go, Em. Two of the local *policía* are on board, as he'll find out soon enough. They'll hold him until someone more senior arrives to deal with him. I just wanted to prevent any further unpleasantness happening on my island.'

They returned to the house, and Jasper explained how his plan had formed and how he'd executed it. While Keith hadn't been so unguarded as to give up the names of his associates, he'd given enough information that the police were sure they'd be able to make further arrests in the near future.

Emily laughed and cried.

Imogen let herself out of the house and made her way along the beach, keeping to the shadows of the palm trees. She should be feeling exultant—and a part of her was. But it also felt as if a line had just been drawn in the sand. It brought home to her the fact that she'd be leaving in four days and would never see Jasper again.

She scrambled up the steep track of the headland at the end of Jasper's beach. Ever since arriving she'd been meaning to climb it. *No time like the present.*

She was breathing hard when she reached the top, but the view rewarded her efforts. A sapphire sea glistened in the sun, ruffled here and there by a playful breeze. That breeze might stiffen later this afternoon, creating whitecaps, but for now it merely caressed and stroked. A few giant rocks rested between the island and the horizon, giving depth and definition to all the amazing blue.

Turning to survey the vista behind, she was greeted with lush greenery. The wooded hill that was Tesoura's interior hid the far coastline from view. Birdcalls rang throughout the forest, hinting at the abundant life hidden there. Below to her left, Eduardo's pride and joy—the garden—reigned in emerald splendour with Jasper's mansion gleaming white and magnificent in the midst of it. Beyond that stretched the lagoon with its tiny dock and barely a ripple disturbed its surface.

If only she could channel some of that tranquillity into her own soul. Finding a flat rock, she sat and stared out to sea. Wasn't there some poet who'd claimed beauty could heal the hurts of the world? She rested her chin on her hands and glared at the glory spread before her, waiting for it to weave its enchantment and magically glue her heart back together.

Stupid heart.

Stupid her for giving it away so easily where it wasn't wanted.

Stupid.

Her eyes burned but she forced her chin up. Falling in love with Jasper wasn't stupid. It seemed almost…inevitable. He was wonderful. Falling in love with him simply went to show what excellent taste she had. It was just a shame he didn't love her back.

She didn't know how long she sat like that before she heard Jasper beating up a path towards her. Cool reason told her it had to be Jasper. Katherine would simply wait until Imogen came down if she wanted to speak to her. Emily would be busy with George, and Eduardo with his garden.

There was nothing cool about how she felt at the thought of seeing him now, though. She tried to school her features. She told herself to be cheerful. She might be in love with a man who didn't love her back, but she still had her pride.

'Hey!' she said, leaping to her feet when he broke through the undergrowth and crested the summit. With a superhuman effort she kept a grin on her face. 'Here's to the man of the moment!' She gave him a round of applause. 'You

were amazing back there—all cool, calm and focussed—like some white knight on his charger.'

'I—'

'I mean—' she knew she was babbling but
couldn't stop '—how good did it feel to slay that
particular dragon?'

'I...'

She skipped forward to high-five him, but
rather than slapping his palm to hers, he caught
her hand, lacing his fingers with hers, and not
letting go. 'You left.'

The hurt in his eyes nearly undid her. She
couldn't tell him the truth—that she'd needed
time alone. She couldn't tell him that in van-
quishing his father he'd forced her to face the
fact that he didn't love her. She could no longer
pretend that he was trapped by his family and
circumstances.

But that was her problem, not his.

His fingers curled around hers as if they'd
never let her go.

Wishful thinking.

Everything inside her throbbed. Her smile
had fled, but she refused to let her chin drop.
'I wanted to give you and Emily some time
alone together. To process all you've managed

to achieve, to celebrate the fact you've broken from your past.'

'You left,' he repeated, his brows lowering over his eyes. 'You don't see it, do you?'

'See what?'

'Without you, Imogen, there wouldn't have been anything to celebrate.'

What was he talking about?

'Without you, I don't want to celebrate.'

Her heart all but stopped.

Jasper swallowed. He'd screwed up, hadn't he?

This lovely woman had offered him a glimpse of another life—a life he desperately wanted—and he'd flung it back at her. She'd offered him her heart. Not in so many words, but they both knew that had been the subtext of their conversation on the beach that night after their kiss.

She'd been prepared to see where things between them might go, but he'd dismissed the idea. Ruthlessly. He winced, imagining how hard-hearted she must've thought him. She'd accepted his rejection with equanimity—hadn't tried to change his mind, had respected his wishes.

And then he'd kissed her again in São Paulo and had rejected her all over again. That had been unforgivable. He didn't blame her for locking her heart up tight against him now.

She pulled her hand from his, her brow wrinkling as if she was trying to make sense of what he'd said. 'I can't take credit for what happened this morning.'

She might've closed her heart to him, but he could open his to her. 'This morning had everything to do with you.' He clenched his hand, trying to keep a hold of the feel of her, wanting it imprinted on his mind. 'If it weren't for you, I might never have believed that Emily was in trouble in the first place.'

'I know you believe that, but I don't. It was you who worked out how to contact her. And when she did make contact, it was you who got her to safety.'

'It was also you,' he pressed on, 'who made me fall in love with George.'

She rolled her eyes. 'I think you'll find George was responsible for that himself.'

'You taught me how to be an uncle.'

It appeared he'd finally shocked her into silence. Her mouth opened, but no words came out.

He widened his stance. 'Yesterday afternoon when my father threatened Emily, I was angry.

When he threatened Katherine, I was outraged. But when he threatened you, I wanted to kill him.'

Even now the memory had everything inside him clenching up tight. 'I knew I could counter the harm he threatened. You all showed me how to do that—and I'd have been happy to do it. But the thought of you having to put up with his spite, being persecuted for no other reason than the fact that you're a good person...' Both his hands clenched. '*That* was the moment I decided to take him down.'

The green highlights in her eyes seemed to alternately flash and dull, like the sun on a moving sea. She moistened her lips and an ache started up inside him. 'Why?'

His mouth dried, but he was through with lies and deceit. 'Because I love you.'

She froze. She blinked. She didn't utter a single damn word.

Give her more, you idiot.

Reaching out, he touched her cheek. 'I know I've given you no reason to believe me—that I've run hot and cold. And I don't blame you if you don't return my feelings, but I can't let you leave this island believing you don't mean anything to me.'

Her lips parted. He wanted to kiss her so badly he started to shake with it. But then she backed up a step and the hope he'd stupidly let loose drained away and the day darkened as if a cloud had just passed across the sun.

He glanced up at the sky. Not a single cloud marred the endless blue—not even on the farthest horizon. Turning back to Imogen, he pressed his lips together to stop from begging her to give him another chance. He didn't regret telling her how he felt; he didn't regret telling her he loved her, but he wouldn't harass her. He'd had enough of men hassling women to last him a lifetime.

She thumped down to a rock as if her legs had given way. She swallowed and gestured to another rock nearby. He took it, hating how much distance it put between them. From here he couldn't reach out and touch her.

That's the point.

'If you'd prefer to be alone, I can leave.'

'I don't want you to leave, I'm just… I know my silence must sound deafening to you, but…' Her eyes narrowed. 'I'm trying to decide if I believe you or not.'

He froze. Did that mean…? Was she saying…? He didn't bother trying to rein in his hope. 'Why do you doubt me?' If he knew that, he might be able to allay it.

She covered her face with her hands, and he understood they weren't playing games here—they were in deadly earnest. 'Because it's what you do, Jasper—it's your modus operandi.' She pulled her hands away. 'You want to protect women... And children.'

She thought that was a bad thing?

'After meeting your father—' she shuddered '—I can see why you don't want to be anything like him.'

He remained quiet, focussed.

'You know that I'm not immune to you. I know you know that.'

His heart pounded.

'And I'm worried that if you think you're hurting me, you'll give me what you think I want regardless of the cost to yourself.'

He leaned towards her. 'You think I'd tell you I loved you to make you happy rather than because it's true?'

Her tongue snaked out to moisten her lips. 'That's the thought that's crossing my mind.'

Damn. He tried not to notice the shine on her lips, tried not to let it distract him. 'You're right insofar as the thought of hurting you makes me feel physically ill.'

Although the sun beat down on them with benevolent warmth, she'd gone pale. His heart gave a sick kick.

'But you're wrong too,' he forced himself to continue. 'I would never lie about loving you. It would hurt you tenfold in the long run because you'd eventually work it out. How could I do that to you—a woman with so much love in her heart and so much joy for life and so much to look forward to?' He shook his head, praying she'd believe him. 'If I thought you loved me, but I didn't return that love—I'd have to tell you. It'd be a clean break. Painful at first, no doubt, but I know you'd move on.'

She blinked.

'That kind of lie—the kind you're accusing me of—is a trap. It'd be a trap for the both of us and I've seen what traps do to people. I don't want that. Not for me. And I sure as hell don't want it for you.'

She rested her elbows on her knees, her chin in her hands as she stared—almost glared—at him. It shifted her towards him fractionally and he wasn't sure if she was aware of that or not.

There had to be some other way he could convince her, something he could—

'You told me that Tesoura is your home. That you have no plans for ever leaving.'

'I was wrong.' He spoke without hesitation. 'Running away like I did was the coward's way out.'

She straightened. 'That's not fair! You had every reason for needing a bolt-hole. You are *not* a coward.'

Her defence warmed him. He wanted to take it as a good sign.

She thrust out her chin. 'And you're not an emotional coward either. You just told me you loved me without knowing if I'd say it back. That was pretty brave.'

He still didn't know if she was going to say it back. But he didn't point that out.

'Regardless of what happens between me and you, Imogen, I'm returning to the real world. I want to be close to my family. I have my heart set on living in Wollongong, but if that's not possible then I'll get a place somewhere in Sydney.'

Her eyes widened at his words.

'I know you don't see it, but you've made me a new man.'

Please let her see that.

'You helped me deal with the bitterness and resentment I'd let fester inside me. But that's not all. You've given me hope.' He wanted her to feel the truth of his words in her bones. 'I'm not talking about the hope that something might happen between the two of us. I'm talking about the hope that I can live a good life again—that I can be an uncle to George, a brother to Emily, a son to my mother, and maybe even a husband and father myself one day. I'm planning to reconnect with the friends I've shunned these last two years, and I'm going to get hands-on again with my business.'

She straightened; her hands pressed to the spot above her heart. Tears sparkled on her lashes.

'You want to know the exact moment I realised I was in love with you?'

She nodded.

'The moment you appeared in the living room in the middle of the night to help me with George when he was teething. I'd never been so darn happy to see anyone. And before you say otherwise, it had nothing to do with George. Seeing you simply made the hard stuff easier to bear. Seeing you made me feel that some piece inside me that had been missing had just been found. I felt...whole.'

Her lips parted.

'When did I *actually* fall in love with you?' He shook his head. 'Probably the moment I saw you dancing with that stupid vacuum cleaner.'

'But…you yelled at me.'

'I didn't yell!' He grimaced. 'Though I was admittedly less than cheerful at the time.'

She kinked an eyebrow at his understatement.

'That was the moment everything started to change, and I didn't want it to. I was pushing back against it, trying to maintain the status quo. I'm sorry I was so bad-tempered. You didn't deserve it.'

The expression in her eyes made his heart beat hard. 'You want to know when I first realised I was in love with you?' she asked.

Every cell inside him fired to life at her words. He tried to keep his feet on the ground, not to get carried away. Her confession didn't mean she still loved him. But her smile…

'It was the moment you made arrangements for me to travel with you and Aunt Katherine to São Paulo. I told you that you were my new favourite person.'

He remembered the exact moment.

'As soon as the words left my mouth, I knew

they were true. I think it all started, though, that day on the beach.'

'When we kissed?'

'No. Though *that* was a revelation.'

She could say that again.

'I'm talking about the day you fell for George. When he grabbed on to you and you just couldn't hold out against him any longer. I think that was the moment when my heart waved a white flag and surrendered.'

But he'd rejected her twice since then. Had he trampled so hard over her heart that she didn't have any love left for him now? He wanted to drop to his knees in front of her but forced himself to remain where he was. 'Imogen, I've just spoken about the future I want. What I want more than anything is for that future to be with you. I don't expect you to trust me immediately.' Desperation clawed at him. 'But please let me see you a little when I'm back in Sydney. Let me prove to you—'

Her smile transformed her face and he couldn't speak as his throat closed over.

'No, Jasper, that's not a deal I want to make.'

But she smiled in a way that lifted rather than felled him.

'The deal is that you see me a lot. *A whole lot.*

Didn't you hear what I just said?' She surged to her feet, and so did he. 'I love you too.' She moved across to stand in front of him, reaching up to touch his face, her eyes soft and her lips even softer. 'I love you.'

And then she was in his arms, her arms wound tight around his neck and her hair tickling his face. He wrapped his arms around her waist and closed his eyes, giving thanks to whatever deity had sent her into his life.

She eased back, her mouth millimetres from his. 'Deal?' she whispered.

'Deal,' he murmured, catching her lips in a kiss that promised a lifetime. He'd finally found the one place he belonged—with Imogen—and he meant to treasure it, to treasure her, forever.

EPILOGUE

Three years later

JASPER GLANCED AROUND the monstrosity of an open-plan kitchen/diner that Katherine had told him was an utter necessity and had to pinch himself. It was crammed to its vaulted ceilings—ceilings Imogen had swooned over—with Christmas cheer, with excited chatter and laughter, and with all the things he'd known Christmas could hold for other people but had never expected to experience for himself.

Several people toasted him as he came into the room and he grinned. It was official—he and Imogen had been added to the Christmas hosting rota. He had to pinch himself again.

His wife hadn't been kidding when she'd said the holiday was a big deal for her family. Tonight, they were hosting the Christmas Eve party; tomorrow Imogen's parents—two of the nicest people he'd ever met—were hosting the traditional all-day Christmas lunch, while the day after that her uncle Robert and aunt Sarah were hosting the Boxing Day wind-down.

And he loved it. All of it. With a passion that almost seemed unholy.

And the house he and Imogen had designed for the ten-acre block of land he'd bought in Wollongong—with its extraordinary ocean views—provided the perfect backdrop for all this warmth and belonging. Everything was...*perfect.*

Almost perfect. His father had another five years to serve on an eight-year jail term, but as far as Jasper could tell not a single person missed him. Aaron had already served his eighteen-month sentence and had relocated to Darwin. Jasper's lips tightened. But only after striking a devil's bargain. In exchange for start-up funds for a bar and restaurant, Aaron had signed away all his custody rights to George. Jasper still couldn't believe the man had suggested such a thing—George was a joy, a delight, a treasure. But if that was the way Aaron felt, then it was better for George to have nothing to do with him.

He pushed the sombre thought away. Tonight was for fun and laughter and giving thanks. Moving behind Imogen, who was putting the finishing touches to a cheese and fruit platter, he slipped his arms about her waist. 'Anything I can do to help?'

She gave a delicious shiver when his lips touched her nape. 'I don't think so—the food's all ready.' They'd prepared a buffet-style feast and had set up picnic tables and blankets on the lawn outside. The evening was balmy and the sky full of oranges, pinks and mauves as the sun started to set. 'But please tell me someone is supervising the children in the pool.'

'Your aunt Fiona and aunt Stacey are keeping a close eye on proceedings while your uncle Jordan and uncle Dennis discuss the merits of different car motors.'

Imogen laughed. 'If they keep that up my aunts might just push them in the deep end.'

'And your cousins are teaching George how to dive.' George, who was nearly four and utterly fearless!

'Good for them.' She set a final bunch of grapes to her platter with a flourish and then turned and looped her arms about his neck. 'So how are you enjoying our very first party in our gorgeous new house?'

'I love it. When can we have another one?'

He didn't try to temper his excitement, his enthusiasm…his joy. He knew it must be shining from his face, but he didn't have to be wary or guarded here—not among these people who'd embraced him and claimed him as one of their own.

Her face softened. 'You deserve all of this, Jasper. All of the fun and holiday spirit and love.'

'I don't know about that.'

'I do,' she said, her voice a soft whisper against his skin.

They'd married eighteen months ago, and he hadn't known it was possible for one man to feel so lucky—loving her was the smartest thing he'd ever done. That love filled his chest now, making him feel weightless, as if he could float up to the highest point of the ceiling.

She glanced beyond him, her luscious lips curving into a smile. 'It's nice to see your mother and Emily enjoying themselves.'

He followed her gaze to the terrace outside, where his mother and sister were firmly ensconced in a circle of Imogen's family—all of them laughing and seemingly talking at once. It'd taken time for the shadows to retreat from their eyes. They'd bear scars forever, he knew that, but it didn't mean they couldn't be happy in the here and now.

He'd had three cottages built on this ten-acre

block, each with its own private garden. Emily and George were in one, Katherine in another, and the married couple he and Imogen had hired as housekeeper and gardener were living in the third. He'd wanted to build one for his mother but she hadn't let him. She'd sold the house in Sydney to buy a modest unit in Wollongong's town centre, within easy access to them all. He hoped that, given enough time, both Emily and his mother would find a love like his and Imogen's—a love that healed and renewed; a love that made the world a place full of hope and possibility.

Imogen reached up on tiptoe to press her lips to his and a familiar surge of heat licked along his veins. Whatever she saw in his face made her chuckle. 'Hold that thought until the party's over.'

He had every intention of doing exactly that. For now, he contented himself with reaching for his phone and selecting a song from his playlist. He spun her in his arms as sixties Southern Californian surf music poured from the speakers. 'Pretend I'm a vacuum cleaner and dance with me.'

She threw her head back and laughed, her dark

curls bouncing with effervescent good humour. 'Best offer I've had all night!'

He made a mental note to better that offer when they were alone.

His heart nearly burst when the entire kitchen and dining room erupted into a storm of dancing. Katherine and Imogen's mother, Gloria, started a complicated dance that had them both breathless by the end and everyone else clapping madly. Katherine's writing career was going from strength to strength and Gloria, in her spare time, had taken it upon herself to become Katherine's marketing manager. He suppressed a grin. So far the arrangement was working beautifully even given the occasional inevitable bump along the way.

'Food's up,' Imogen hollered when the song ended.

They ate. They socialised. They sang Christmas carols for the children. At nine o'clock the fireworks he'd arranged—with all the associated council permits and fire safety precautions in place—created a magical display that delighted child and adult alike.

After that, sleepy children were put to sleep in spare bedrooms or on the sofas in the lounge room while the adults continued to revel for another couple of hours. Eventually, though, the guests started to excuse themselves. Jasper saw the last of them off and then wandered back through the house to find his glorious wife.

She stood outside on the terrace, staring at a moonlit sea. She turned to greet him with a smile as big as her heart, and full of love. For him. The knowledge awed him. 'That was one of the best Christmas Eve parties ever, Jasper. If we're not careful we might just find ourselves hosting it every year.'

'I wouldn't mind.'

She poked him in the ribs before sliding an arm about his waist. 'You'd *love* it.'

He grinned, tucking her in more firmly against his side. 'That was the best Christmas Eve ever.'

'Which is what you said last year...and the year before that,' she teased.

'And I'll probably say it again next year.' He sobered, glancing down at her. 'They keep getting better. I don't know how, but they do.'

She sobered too. Moving out from beneath his arm, she took his hand in both her own. 'I think this one is extra special.'

'It's the first time we've hosted one of the Christmas events.' *That* was a big deal. 'And we did it in our dream home.' To be honest, though, wherever Imogen happened to be was his definition of dream home.

'Not just that—this whole year has been amazing.'

Her and Lauren's sewing business had become a soaring success. They now ran a very exclusive fashion house—The House of Tesoura. Emily had started her own PR company, and the fashion house had been her first client. Both businesses were thriving. 'You've achieved amazing things this year, Imogen. The House of Tesoura is the toast of the town.'

'I'm ecstatic about that, of course—' her eyes danced '—and over the moon that I can blow raspberries at all of the naysayers, but that's not what I'm talking about. I'm talking about the plans we discussed a few months ago. I feel as if we're on the cusp of an exciting new adventure.'

He swallowed and his heart started to thud. 'You mean…about starting a family soon?' He was almost too afraid to hope. He already had so much.

'That's exactly what I'm talking about.' She bit her lip and then took his hand and laid it flat against her abdomen, her eyes shining and her lips trembling.

A jolt shot through him like electricity—he

went rigid, and then a wild, glorious excitement coursed through him. 'You're…?'

She nodded. 'I found out yesterday. I wasn't going to tell you until tomorrow. I thought it'd be the best Christmas present ever. But I've been bursting with the news…and now seemed like the perfect time.'

He couldn't push a single word past the lump in his throat.

Imogen was pregnant.

His hand curved against her in wonder.

They were going to have a baby.

'Happy?' she whispered.

With a superhuman effort, he swallowed down the lump. 'I thought I was happy two minutes ago. This—' he shook his head '—it's almost too much.'

'No, it's not, darling Jasper.' She reached up to touch his face. 'It's just right. It's exactly as it should be.'

'I'm the luckiest man alive.' Cupping her face, he lowered his mouth to hers and told her in a language that needed no words exactly how happy he was.

* * * * *

LET'S TALK
Romance

For exclusive extracts, competitions
and special offers, find us online:

f facebook.com/millsandboon

⊙ @millsandboonuk

🐦 @millsandboon

Or get in touch on 0844 844 1351*

For all the latest titles coming soon,
visit millsandboon.co.uk/nextmonth

Want even more
ROMANCE?

Join our bookclub today!

THE MAID, THE
MILLIONAIRE
AND THE BABY